DEATH IN THE DISTILLERY

Other books by Kent Conwell:

Gunfight at Frio Canyon
The Riddle of Mystery Inn
An Eye for an Eye
A Hanging in Hidetown
Skeletons of the Atchafalaya
Galveston
The Gambling Man
Red River Crossing
A Wagon Train for Brides
Friday's Station
Sidetrip to Sand Springs
The Alamo Trail
Blood Brothers
The Gold of Black Mountain
Glitter of Gold
The Ghost of Blue Bone Mesa
Texas Orphan Train
Painted Comanche Tree
Valley of Gold
Bumpo, Bill, and the Girls
Wild Rose Pass
Cattle Drive to Dodge

DEATH IN THE DISTILLERY

●

Kent Conwell

AVALON BOOKS
NEW YORK

PRINTED IN THE UNITED STATES OF AMERICA
ON ACID-FREE PAPER
BY HADDON CRAFTSMEN, BLOOMSBURG, PENNSYLVANIA

To Judy, a friend for twenty-nine years,
my secretary for twenty-seven.
And to Gayle, my wife.
The only one who knows more
of my shortcomings than Judy.

Chapter One

The first real case I ever worked on for Blevins' Investigations was in 1998, the year of El Niño. It was the year weathermen had to admit their profession was more of a crapshoot than a science. It was a year of choking dust storms, idyllic spring days, paralyzing ice blizzards, warm nights perfumed with honeysuckle, deadly mud slides, gentle rains, and searing droughts followed by killer floods. Nature had lost her sense of proportion.

So, I shouldn't have been surprised when a chopped up body resembling steak tartare dropped at my feet, and I was paid four hundred bucks a day to prove it was an accident.

The past two weeks in central Texas had been a conundrum of meteorological confusion. Sunny forecasts brought torrential rains. Cloudy forecasts brought out the scorching Texas sun. Naturally, the weatherman claimed the unpredictable weather was a result of El Niño.

In Austin, Texas, fourteen seniors at Madison High School failed economics and naturally, their parents denounced El Niño.

Six state legislators were caught in prostitution stings on the downtown streets of Austin. They claimed El Niño made them do it.

1

The weather phenomenon caught the blame for everything from bad hair to burned steak. Even my next door neighbor, a lecherous Texas Aggie—I think that's probably redundant—blamed El Niño when his wife caught him and a pickup bimbo in the back seat of a car out behind our apartments.

Later that night, he knocked on my door. I pretended to be asleep. The poor guy only wanted a place to flop, but the truth was that while I judged no one's personal life, I wasn't foolish enough to step right into the middle of a donnybrook. Let them fight it out in the streets was my motto.

Finally, El Niño played its trump card when Janice Coffman-Morrison, my on-again, off-again Significant Other called, wanting me to escort her to her great aunt's annual reception at Chalk Hills Distillery. From that moment on, my life changed.

I wasn't crazy about attending the reception, for I viewed those gatherings as merely showplaces for the socially challenged to take another step up the ladder of social snobbery. On the other hand, I seldom turned down the offer of free food and drink. But to be truthful, one compliment I had to pay Chalk Hills Distillery was that no expense was spared on the annual receptions. This one promised to be even more extravagant because, according to Thomas Floria, the wine columnist for the *Austin Daily Press*, Beatrice Morrison, Chalk Hills CEO, was anxious to host a lavish event that would drive her company stock higher.

Janice insisted I accompany her. I protested I didn't have the time, but she knew better. I was a private investigator, a skiptracer, which is really just a missing person locator, and the missing person business had been slow of late. Runaways and skips must have decided to stay in place because of the debilitating heat or the whimsical vagaries of El Niño.

Anyway, I pleaded that my aquarium needed a good cleaning, but Janice reminded me that she had performed that task herself, just the week before.

That's when she began pouting. "After all, Tony," she whined, "how will it look if the niece of the owner shows up without an escort?"

Janice was a professional pouter. She had the technique down to a science. Pouting 101. I had no doubt that course was the prerequisite for each of the required social classes in the curriculum for the Very Rich at all the exclusive finishing schools in Atlanta and Dallas, which she had attended.

And for the thousandth time, the feminine artifice worked. I sighed, and stared at the aquarium, envying Oscar, my tiny albino Tiger Barb, who reminded me of a pink penny with fins.

Oscar, as was his habit, glided in lazy circles through the plastic water sprite and Amazon sword plants all by his lonesome. He was the lone survivor of the murderous chemical attack by Jack Edney. "Okay, what time is the reception?"

"One, but I want to go early so I can spend some time with Aunt Beatrice. After all, I'm the only family she has left, and the poor dear is so lonesome."

I bit my tongue. Beatrice Lenore Morrison was many things, but lonesome wasn't one of them. Ever since her husband died from a massive heart attack fifteen years earlier and left her Chalk Hills Distillery, Beatrice had gone out of her way not to be lonely. She practiced discretion, but among the socially elite of Austin, gossip spread like groping hands beneath a blanket. Nobody admitted it, but everyone enjoyed it. "Pick you up at eleven then. That'll give you a couple of hours with your aunt before the reception."

"Good. We'll use my Miata."

I didn't argue. She hated riding in my Chevy pickup. It rode rough and rattled like gravel in a beer can. The air conditioning operated on its own whimsy, usually when the weather was freezing. Like a recalcitrant child, the AC unit picked its times to function, and since it had regularly demonstrated an obvious aversion to hot weather, I usually drove with the window down.

Besides, the little Miata was fun to drive.

By eleven o'clock, the temperature was nearing ninety. To say the day promised to be a warm one was a consummate understatement.

Wearing a prim skirt and lace-collared blouse with a matching vest, Janice was standing beside the Miata outside her townhouse when I drove up. She flashed me a bright smile and, giving her short brown hair a toss, climbed in the passenger's side of the red convertible with the white leather interior. I slipped behind the wheel, buckled up, tilted my chin at a rakish angle, and slammed the little car into gear.

Normally, the winding drive along Bee Tree Road through the oak and cedar-covered hills west of Austin was pleasant and relaxing, but for some reason, a pinprick of uneasiness nagged at me. When we topped the last hill and looked down on the collection of white stucco buildings with bright red roofs of Spanish tile that made up Chalk Hills, I spotted a figure running from a large barn. He raced toward a lone woman who stood under a huge oak between the distillery and a plowed field. Serpentine limbs thick as barrels spread in all directions, from the field to the roof of the distillery.

My uneasy feeling quickly escalated into a chilling apprehension.

I stared in disbelief at the pile of flesh and cloth in the shallow ditch, uncertain if it were a man or woman. But, whoever or whatever it had been, it was dead. A set of tandem discs behind a tractor takes no prisoners and gives no second chances.

The cleft in the back of the skull through which brains bulged grinned at me like a Halloween ghoul. "Jesus. Who . . . who is it?"

"That, Mr. Boudreaux, was Emmett Patterson," Beatrice

Morrison, matriarch of the Chalk Hills Distillery, stated with cold disinterest. Her shoulders square, her spine stiff, she stared indifferently upon what had once been a human being, at the same time idly brushing at the dust collecting on her dark brown business jacket. Her thin lips curled in distaste.

The man standing beside her had the face of a bulldog.

Leaning against my left arm, Janice gagged and buried her face in my shoulder. My sport jacket was freshly cleaned, and I hoped she didn't stain it.

A lumbering man who reminded me of a gorilla brushed past Janice and me. "Oh, my Lord," he muttered in a thin, girlish voice. Another man hurried up to us. His hair was long and greasy.

Across the recently disked field, a Massey Ferguson tractor lay halfway overturned in a ditch, held in place by the heavy discs to which it was hitched. Clods of dirt clung to the round, steel blades.

I glanced at the three men. I figured they were employees of the distillery. Beyond them, the door in the side of the distillery opened and a well-dressed man strode toward us. I recognized him from the newspapers. William Cleyhorn, a local Austin shark, I mean, attorney.

Janice muttered into my shoulder, "I feel dizzy."

"Take a deep breath," I replied, grateful for the shade of the ancient oak under which we stood. I heard a faint thud and glanced around. Through an open spot in the crown of the oak, I glimpsed a face peering down from a window on the second floor of the distillery. After a few moments surveying the scene below, the face vanished.

One thing for sure, I told myself, looking back at what was beginning to resemble steak tartare without peppers or onions, by no stretch of the imagination could El Niño be blamed for the death of Emmett Patterson.

Behind me, tires crunched to a halt in the gravel. I glanced over my shoulder.

Police Sergeant Ben Howard paused as he opened the car door and frowned when he spotted me. He slammed the door and strode in my direction, his ubiquitous cigar jammed in his mouth. "What are you doing here, Boudreaux?" He had a way of growling when he spoke.

"Believe it or not, Sergeant, I'm a guest." I introduced him to Janice, whom I was supporting to keep her from collapsing. "Can I take her inside? She isn't feeling too well."

He eyed me a moment, then grunted, "Not yet." But his tone softened when he realized I wasn't sticking my nose into his business. "What happened?" He turned toward the remains of Emmett Patterson.

"Beats me." I nodded to the tractor across the field. "Looks like he fell off the tractor and under the discs."

Howard grimaced. "Reminds me of the hamburger meat my wife fed me last night."

Janice gagged. "Hambur . . . oh, God, Tony. I . . . I feel sick." I tightened my arm about her waist.

"Hold on," I encouraged her. "I'll get you some water."

A voice behind us spoke up. "He wasn't supposed to work today." The nasal twang belonged to one of the employees, a throwback to the flower children of the sixties and seventies. Long greasy hair, sallow complexion, and sunken cheeks, he wore a sweat-stained Houston Astros ball cap.

The man's words piqued my curiosity. I forgot about the water for Janice.

Howard frowned at him. "Who are you?"

"Claude Hawkins. I work here. Mrs. Morrison gave us the day off. Emmett wasn't supposed to be working. We was going into town after cleaning up the place when the reception was over."

"Cleaning up the place? I thought you said he wasn't supposed to be working." Howard glared at him.

"I meant not on the tractor. We finished the field a couple of days ago. We was supposed to let it lay fallow."

Despite his grating personality and deliberate bad manners, Sergeant Ben Howard was a thorough and determined investigator. Whether it was fraud, theft, or murder, his bulldog tenacity closed every case he handled.

Maybe if I'd been more of an investigator like the sergeant, Blevins' Investigations wouldn't have stuck me in missing persons, and given the choice assignments to its top sleuth, Al Grogan. That was one of the reasons I appreciated Oscar, my little Tiger Barb. I knew what it felt like to swim in circles.

Janice groaned. "Tony, I mean it. I think . . . I'm going to be sick."

"Okay. We'll get some water. Just a second." I loosened her lace collar and glanced around for the nearest water.

Howard studied the dead man. A frown wrinkled his forehead, and he touched the toe of his scuffed shoe to the polished chukka boot on Emmett Patterson's severed foot. Green flies swirled and buzzed. "Doesn't look like he planned on much work today."

A shorter, heavily muscled man stepped forward. His arms hung down at his sides from rounded shoulders. He reminded me of a gorilla. "He did that sometimes, Sergeant. I mean, worked in his good clothes." His voice was high and thin. I cringed. The voice and body didn't match.

"Who are you?" Howard frowned.

"Seldes. Tom Seldes. I'm the rackhouse foreman. I saw Emmett this morning before he picked up the tractor. I guess he was going to run the disc before the reception."

Janice tried to pull away from me. "I think I'm going to faint."

Howard glanced at me and nodded. I hurried Janice to the main house, which was of the same Spanish architecture as the distillery and the cottages. A series of arches supported the portico around the perimeter of the mansion.

At least, it was a mansion to me. Anything larger than two bedrooms and a bath, I considered a mansion. Inside, the servants took over, quickly ushering her from the foyer down a carpeted hall and behind a set of double doors. The bedroom, I figured.

* * *

Back outside, the sun baked the countryside. The stench of Emmett Patterson ripened the air. Fat, green flies swarmed the scene, buzzing frantically. Crazy how the human mind works, but I couldn't help noticing the varying pitch of their tiny wings, some high and thin, others more of a growl.

I moved upwind of the shredded body. The mixture of offal and blood was beginning to fill the air with a sickening piquancy, not conducive to the upcoming buffet being laid out on the grounds.

The coroner and his crime scene boys were taking pictures, measurements, and all the minute but essential bits and pieces of an investigation that helped determine the outcome of the case, for good or bad. Ben Howard, the unlit cigar stub bobbing between his lips, continued talking to everyone present, taking notes, asking questions, and muttering under his breath.

I remained in the background, more out of morbid curiosity than for any other reason.

An hour later, Howard closed his notebook, slipped it back into his pocket, and watched as the meat wagon carried off the remains of Emmett Patterson. I hoped the Medical Examiner was a jigsaw puzzle whiz. He was in for a world-class challenge when the ME techs dropped the corpse off at the forensics lab.

After the ambulance disappeared over the hill in a boil of dust, Howard glanced at me. He shrugged and moved my way. "Heck of a way to go, huh?" He lit his cigar, took a deep drag, and blew out a column of blue smoke. "I was heading back to the station when we got the word." He shook his head. "I wish the citizens would give us a break."

I grunted, and we both continued staring after the ambulance, which had long since disappeared. A male thing, I guess, speaking of violent death with the same nonchalance reserved for casual chitchat, and staring into space so we wouldn't have to look at each other.

I shrugged. "Accidents happen."

He snorted. "So they say."

Something in his tone made me look around. "It was an accident, wasn't it?" My brain suddenly came alive with all sorts of insidious scenarios.

"Yeah. Looks that way. We'll let the technicians at the lab check it out, but that's what I figure. Probably copped some of the free booze the old broad was going to hand out. Got himself snockered and decided he was Jeff Gordon or Mario Andretti doing the Chalk Hills Five Hundred. There's disc cuts in the ditch. He probably hit the ditch, lost his balance because of the booze, and fell off the tractor seat."

"Maybe he hit his head on one of the limbs when he went under the tree." I indicated the spreading limbs of the oak.

Howard shrugged. "Maybe. They seem a little high though. Anyway. We'll see what the ME says." He hitched up his pants. "Well, see you around, Boudreaux. Keep your nose clean."

Which meant stay out of his way. "No sweat, Sergeant."

I went back to see about Janice, but the butler stopped me in the foyer and ushered me into the walnut-paneled library. When I entered, Beatrice Morrison rose from behind a massive Victorian desk longer than my Chevrolet pickup, her thin body ramrod straight, her bearing regal. She would have made a striking Cleopatra. Well, maybe one gone to seed somewhat, but still, she exuded a majesty, an intimidating sovereignty that filled the room with a palpable reverence that somehow made me feel like I should kneel and bow.

She fixed her icy blue eyes on mine and flicked them toward a paunchy, silver-haired man on the leather couch. "You know my attorney, William Cleyhorn."

"Mr. Cleyhorn." I gave him a brief nod, noting the expensive suit he wore. Probably either a Givenchy or Charles Jourdan. Maybe even a Brioni. Me, I'm a Sears man, though not by choice. I could easily learn to live with a

Givenchy or Jourdan. A Brioni, at two to seven thousand a shot, I don't even dream about.

He arched an eyebrow.

I'd always heard that the rich had subtle means of communication. If a single arched eyebrow meant hello, what would both of them mean?

She came right to the point. "The police have departed?"

"Yes."

"And? Was it an accident?"

I hesitated, for a moment taken aback by her question. I never dreamed the Cleopatra of Austin Society would consider Emmett Patterson's death anything other than an accident. And, inexplicably, the very fact she posed the question made me curious, one of my lesser bad habits. "Yes. Any reason to think otherwise?"

Her eyes seemed to drill into my own as she mulled my reply. Finally, she spoke, ignoring my question. "Mr. Boudreaux. You and my grandniece have a relationship."

Somehow, when she said the word relationship, it sounded unsanitary. "Well, sort of."

"As a result, I feel I can be quite candid with you."

I frowned. Where was this taking us? "Sure, Mrs. Morrison. Be as frank as you want."

She glanced at Cleyhorn, then tilted her chin. Her voice grew hard. "I want you to gather incontrovertible evidence that Emmett Patterson's death was an accident. Enough evidence to prove he was not murdered."

Chapter Two

Cleyhorn half raised his hand, then dropped it as I stared at her, unsure of my hearing. The lemony smell of furniture polish, mixed with the subtle musk of leather, filled the room. "Not murdered?" Puzzled, I glanced at Cleyhorn, then cut my eyes back to Beatrice Morrison. "But, I just told you the police think it was an accident. Besides, how can I prove someone wasn't murdered?"

She looked at me as if I was a fretful child. "If you can prove a person was murdered, then surely you can prove one wasn't murdered."

I had the feeling I had just awakened from a dream, only to find myself in another dream. What's the old joke, deja vu all over again? "Isn't the police report enough?"

"My attorney, Mr. Cleyhorn, and I are very concerned of the impact the accident could have upon company stock. There are millions at stake." She paused, sighed at my obvious confusion, and explained. "Chalk Hills Distillery is a high profile corporation. We have reached this point by always being proactive, not reactive. We cannot afford any lingering publicity, which might possibly drive stock prices down. Even a dollar loss per share translates into millions. Now, do you understand why it is so important that the matter be handled quickly and efficiently?"

I frowned. Her request didn't make sense, which in turn

11

Kent Conwell

made me even more curious. "Seems like you need a public relations firm instead of a private investigator. I can't do any more than the police. And a good PR firm could handle the damage control on this without any problem." I shrugged and added, "Not that there is much damage to the company at all. At least, the way I see it. Hey, the guy fell off the tractor and got himself killed."

William Cleyhorn stepped forward, carefully buttoning his coat over his vest as if he was addressing a jury. His voice was rich, booming with courtroom resonance, but the sly look in his eyes still gave the impression of being only one gene removed from the evolutionary chain of a snake. "Perhaps I should explain it to the young man, Beatrice."

Her tone grew testy. "Then hurry, William. We must begin the reception on time. You did say the police have departed, didn't you, Tony?"

"Yes, ma'am."

She looked at Cleyhorn. "Be sure you instruct our people to clean up where that horrid body lay. And put out some sort of spray to kill the odor. I don't want any of our guests to be offended."

He gave her a nod of deference. "All is well, Beatrice. They know their job. They'll take care of it." He turned back to me, continuing in a gentle, condescending tone reserved for idiots and morons. "You see, Tony. Often, the validity of investigations by the local police is called into question. By initiating our own thorough, impartial, and expeditious investigation, we hope to alleviate any fears or concerns our stockholders might experience regarding the continued success of the company. In effect, we are proclaiming to the world that we have nothing to hide, nothing to fear, that indeed this unfortunate incident was simply a horrible accident. Horrible indeed," he added for effect.

I remembered a line in *Hamlet* from my days when I struggled to teach English to high school kids who didn't want to learn, in schools that didn't want me to teach. *The lady doth protest too much, methinks.* Seemed to me, both were protesting too much. I chided myself for being so cynical, but cynicism and curiosity were two of the several reasons that drove me from teaching, and then out of the insurance business. Teaching was frustrating, and insurance, boring. "I see what you're saying, but I'm no public relations hound, and I can't see how my investigation would carry any more weight than the opinion of the police. To be honest, I think it would be a waste of my time and your money."

Cleyhorn sniffed. "You're right, of course. But it is to the corporation's advantage to have a supporting report from an outside party, a . . . ah, disinterested party." He paused to glance at Beatrice, who seemed to be staring right through me. "You see, Tony, we need documentation from you, or someone like you, to assuage the apprehension of the board and the stockholders."

Then he turned into the kindly uncle. His voice grew syrupy. "If you believe it to be a waste of time, then why don't you let me help you out by having my secretary type up a simple, little report stating that after speaking with so and so, and doing so on and so forth . . . you have made the determination supporting the Medical Examiner's conclusion that . . ." He glanced at Beatrice. "What was the man's name?"

"Emmett Patterson," she replied tersely.

"Oh, yes. That you have determined Emmett Patterson's death was an accident. Something like that. That way, we have the statement we want for the board, and for the press. On top of that, you are eight hundred dollars ahead." He hesitated. "I think fifty dollars an hour is the going rate. That's for two days."

Tempting offer. I considered it. All it really amounted to was eight hundred bucks for a signature, my signature on a document stating what I already believed. Of course, I knew why she wanted me to carry out the investigation. Janice. What else? And the fact that because of Janice, they guessed I would probably say exactly what they wanted.

I tried to ignore the curiosity burning a hole in my brain, but I couldn't shake it. I met Cleyhorn's amused gaze.

"Okay. I'll do it, but the way I should. I can't take your
money for just signing my name. Give me those couple
days. Get me a list of everyone who worked with Emmett
Patterson. I'll talk to them, and I'll have my report on your
desk Wednesday morning by eight o'clock."

He nodded and looked at Beatrice. She drew her shoulders back stiffly. "I know I can count on your discretion,
should it become necessary, Tony," she added.

Before I had a chance to wonder about the discretion
angle, she glanced at Cleyhorn, gave her head a regal tilt
and said, "Come, William. We mustn't be late for the reception."

The paneled walnut door opened and Janice stuck her
head inside. She smiled weakly, her face still pale. "Aunt
Beatrice. Are you all right?"

Beatrice Morrison smiled at her grandniece, a smile as
thin as a razor blade. "Yes, dear. Tony and I have been
visiting."

Janice gave me a weak, grateful smile, then hurried
across the carpeted room to hug her aunt. Despite her earlier distress, Janice did not have a hair out of place, nor a
wrinkle in her outfit. To paraphrase Fitzgerald, the rich are
not like the average guy.

I watched the two embrace, wondering what percentage
of her aunt's genes Janice possessed. I'd always heard that
if you want to see what your wife will look like twenty
years from now, look at your mother-in-law. Did that time-
worn aphorism apply to aunts also?

Emmett Patterson's death did nothing to detract from the
gaiety of the reception. Booze flowed, hors d'oeuvres vanished, gossip spread, and innuendo prevailed.

Janice stayed at her aunt's elbow, which left me to fend
for myself as usual. That inborn indifference through which
the rich viewed the lower classes was another reason our
relationship seemed to be going in circles like my little
Tiger Barb, Oscar.

We met a few years back when I was helping her out of

an insurance jam. I wasn't interested in getting serious, but we had fun together even though I quickly realized I was simply a dependable escort, an infrequent lover, an occasional confidant.

In other words, I was a tool to satisfy her needs. And she was the same for me. We had reconciled our positions in our relationship. And both of us were fairly content.

Inexplicably, despite the skewed relationship between us, we were very good friends who enjoyed each other's company. From time to time, Janice spoke of "our relationship." After a few of those little discussions, which I really didn't understand, I learned when to agree and when not to agree.

The Chalk Hills reception went the way it was supposed to go. Drinks were plentiful, and the tables were laden with platters of deli sandwiches, vegetables, and a variety of exotic appetizers, most of which I wouldn't touch on a dare. Dishes that could double for fish bait did nothing for my palate.

I followed the redneck route. I grabbed a straight bourbon and dropped a few party spirals on my lead crystal dish, a sample from each platter, turkey and pepperjack, ham and swiss, and red pepper and olive, all rolled with herbed cream cheese and spinach in tasty bread.

The size of a half-dollar, the spirals were enough to dull the appetite. Still, I would have preferred a platter of crawfish etouffee or jambalaya, rib-sticking fare from my Louisiana roots. While I sat licking the cream cheese off my fingers, I promised myself to whip up a gumbo in spite of the hot weather.

Chicken and sausage were the only decent Cajun gumbo that could be prepared from local ingredients this side of Port Arthur, Texas, which has so many emigrant Cajuns from Louisiana that residents claim the city is the capital of southwestern Louisiana, and Baton Rouge be hanged.

Just after my mother and I moved to Austin, she whipped up a shrimp and oyster gumbo using local ingredients. We both gagged. The only shrimp available had been locally

frozen, and imparted a disgusting flavor somewhere between sea water and vinegar. It was like eating salty soup
with chunks of rubber floating in it. After only a portion
of one bowl, she dumped the remainder down the disposal.

A couple of times a year when we visited home, we'd
bring Louisiana ingredients back with us. After Mom
moved back to Church Point, I continued doing the same.
Now, I return with two or three quarts of oysters and fifty
or so pounds of shrimp, fresh from the bayou and gulf,
which I clean and freeze myself. I also bring in three boxes
of smoked sausages. Then, whenever I wish, I can have a
fine pot of shrimp and oyster or chicken and sausage
gumbo, spicy enough to drain the sinuses, delectable
enough to encourage a second or third bowl, and satisfying
enough to put a body into a sound sleep.

During the drive back to Austin after the reception, Janice questioned me about my conversation with her aunt. I
told her of her aunt's proposition. "I still think the idea is
foolish, but if it will make her feel better, I'll do it."

"Will it take long?" She stared into her compact mirror,
straightening her brown pageboy and smoothing her
makeup.

"Couple of days. I'm only going to talk to those who
worked with Patterson. Cleyhorn gave me their names before we left the reception. There's probably twenty or so
employees who had nothing to do with him, who never saw
him, who weren't there today. I'm not going to waste my
time or her money on them. To be honest, I'm just going
through the motions. Everything I do, the police have done.
Besides, it's an easy way to pick up eight big ones."

"Tony! You should be ashamed." Her eyes twinkled in
merriment.

"For what?" I glanced sidelong at her. "Your aunt has
more money than the Bank of England. I told her hiring
me was foolish, but she insisted. If anything, I should resent
her." I suppressed a grin.

Janice's merriment faded. "Resent? Aunt Beatrice? But why?" She leaned forward and stared at me, perplexed.

"Why, for prostituting me. I'm selling her my time just so she can feel better." A grin broke across my lips.

Janice leaned back against the seat and chuckled. "You're teasing me. Just you wait. I'll get even."

"Yeah? Well, I might just decide to take out my fee in trade."

Her cheeks colored. She ducked her head. "Tony! You're shameless."

"Yeah. I know."

Sometimes, Janice and I really hit off.

She scooted around in the seat. "If you're not busy tonight, why don't you go to the Travis County day lily exhibit with me?"

A day lily exhibit? My brain scrambled for a way to beg off. "No, thanks. I think I need to do a little research on distilleries before tomorrow." It was a flimsy excuse, but the best I could do on short notice. I was never a very imaginative person. Stubborn, but not too imaginative.

With a shrug, she turned back to the front. "Okay. Maybe next time."

That evening, I called Marty Blevins, my boss at Blevins' Investigations. He made it plain when he hired me that he did have some reservations over my inexperience, but since I'd pulled him out of a burning car, he felt obligated to give me a shot.

I glanced out of my apartment window as I briefed Marty on the assignment, the expectations, and the pay. A car was parked at the curb across the street. A cigarette glowed in the growing dusk.

"Sounds screwy to me, Tony. Sure you can handle it? You've never done any real investigative work." He stressed the word "real."

I forgot about the car. "Hey, look Marty. I'm no Sherlock Holmes or your super sleuth Grogan, but even I can ask a few questions. This is just a routine matter that can be wrapped up in a couple of days at the most. Besides, I'm tired of just running down bond jumpers or runaway kids. I deserve a chance to prove I'm more than a kid chaser."

He didn't reply for several seconds. I heard a sigh. "Okay. Make me proud."

I clenched my teeth. That was his departing remark to everyone: *Make me proud.* Like a father. I often wondered if he said it to his son when the boy took the throne in the bathroom. *Make me proud, son. Yeah, Dad. I'll make you proud.*

"Sure, Marty. Don't worry. Everything will be fine."

After I hung up, I splashed a jelly glass half full of Jim Beam Black Label Bourbon, my preference to the Chalk Hills Sour Mash, and downed it in one gulp, seething at the implication in his words. *Sure you can handle it?* I poured another glass and plopped down on the couch in front of the TV. So I wasn't one of his aces, or even one of his top half-dozen aces. All this job called for was compiling information already volunteered.

Still, in all fairness, Marty had taken a chance on me. The only background I brought to the company was as an insurance adjuster with very little investigative experience and a school-teacher experienced at dodging bullets and knives. On the other hand, he knew all that when he hired me.

I closed my eyes and leaned my head back on the couch. I was depressed. My career as a PI was going nowhere. Like Oscar. Around and around and around. When my old man bailed out on Mom and me, he said the two of us were just Louisiana trash. Never amount to a thing. Maybe the old man was right. Maybe I should have stayed in teaching. I sure wasn't bowling anyone over as a private investigator.

Through the thin walls of my apartment, I heard my Aggie chum and his wife, Nora, engaging in their nightly shouting match. Marriage. That was one entanglement I'd managed to escape without any permanent damage.

Diane and I were high school sweethearts in Church Point, even after I moved with my mother to Austin when

I was in the eleventh grade. She and I started at the University of Texas together, but she dropped out, and we drifted apart. Several years later, we got back together. Unlike most of our friends who made one baby after another because they believed it was their God-given mission to procreate the entire world all by themselves, Diane and I had no offspring and, within two years, the thrill of lust and passion faded when we had to wake up each morning and face each other at our worst.

The best thing I can say about Diane is we parted amicably. She took her clothes, the furniture, the car, and I took my clothes, a ten-gallon aquarium with Oscar, his swimming mates, and a cab. Like the old country song from way back, "She Got the Gold Mine, and I Got the Shaft." But I never regretted the split at all. I was satisfied with Oscar and his cohorts, a few Tiger and Checker Barbs.

Once, I'd put some Angelfish in with the Barbs, but the little Barbs chased the docile little Angels around the aquarium, nipping at their fins. The Angels would probably have died from heart attacks if Jack Edney hadn't come along.

Next thing I knew, cold liquid soaked my lap. I jumped up, realizing I'd dozed off and spilled my drink. "Jesus." I grumbled as I swiped a dishtowel across the wet couch. "Get to bed, Tony. You're wasting good booze."

I glanced out the window as I started to the bedroom. The car was still by the curb, and using all my powers of deduction, I theorized someone was in the car because a cigarette was still glowing. I spoke aloud. "How's that, Marty? Pretty good detecting, huh?"

Moments after I turned off the lights, I heard a car engine roar to life. Throwing back the covers, I peered out the window. The car had disappeared. With a frown, I climbed back into bed, wondering if I was being watched. I chided myself. "Who would want to keep an eye on you?"

A pounding on my door awakened me. Drowsily, I peered at the digital clock. Two-thirty. The pounding continued. "What the . . ."

I staggered to my feet, grabbed my robe, and by the light of the aquarium, made my way to the door. I flipped on the porch light and peered through the peephole. Talk about coincidence. My old teaching buddy, and fish killer without compare, Jack Edney, stood gazing forlornly at the door. He looked like he'd been stomped on, spit at, and squeezed dry.

"Jesus, Jack," I said, opening the door. "What are you doing out at this time of night?" The sweet-sour stench of alcohol blasted me square in the face. "You look terrible. You drunk?"

He swayed unsteadily, a silly smirk plastered on his thin face. "I . . . I sure hope so." He slurred his words. "Can I sleep here tonight, Tony?"

When I hesitated, he continued. "Maggie threw me out."

I considered my options, which at two-thirty in the morning were severely limited. "She's not going to come over and tear the place apart, is she? My landlady doesn't like any disturbances."

"Naw. She doesn't know where I am." Tears gathered in his eyes. His tone grew maudlin. "Probably doesn't care either."

With a sigh, I stepped back. Last thing I needed was for some lush to go on a crying jag on my front porch at two-thirty in the morning. "Yeah. Come on in. You know where the couch is. Lock the door behind you. And stay away from the aquarium. You killed all my fish except one, and now he only swims in circles."

Jack hung his head. "I told you, Tony. I didn't mean to take a leak in the aquarium. I thought it was the john."

Jack was still sleeping when I left the next morning, and Oscar, my diminutive Barb, was still alive. Jack must have found the bathroom. Thank God for small miracles.

Chapter Three

Bright and early meant 8 A.M. to me, but bright and early meant 5 A.M. to the employees at Chalk Hills Distillery. The mechanic, David Runnels, was squatting next to the open doors of the maintenance barn with a cup of coffee in one hand and a cigarette in the other when I pulled up in front.

Inside the spacious metal building sat the bright red Massey Ferguson tractor, a monster 230, showroom clean. A nearby bay held the tandem discs, a forward gang and a backward gang that looked like an elongated X. At either end of the X was a seven-foot wing folded vertically. Extended horizontally, the disc stretched thirty feet from end to end, thirty feet of concave disc blades shiny as new steel and designed to slice nine inches into hard earth like a scalpel through flesh.

I remembered the hours I had spent on tractors back in Louisiana helping my grandfather. No fun.

Several other vehicles were parked in the barn, all bright red with the white logo of Chalk Hills Distillery on the doors.

Runnels arched an eyebrow in that bulldog face of his, but I had the feeling the message he was sending me wasn't the same kind of greeting as Lawyer Cleyhorn.

He looked me up and down as I climbed out of my

pickup. Maybe my jeans and sport coat didn't seem the appropriate dress for a private investigator, or maybe he was just naturally surly.

He rose slowly. In a gravelly voice, he said. "Mrs. Morrison said you'd be out today. Told us to cooperate. So, I'm cooperating. Make it fast. I got work to do."

"We all got work to do, Mr. Runnels," I shot back, irritated by his curt greeting. "In fact, we're both getting paid to do what Mrs. Morrison wants."

He understood the implication in my words. His black eyes flicked nervously about the grounds. "What do you want to know?"

"Out here? Or do you want to go inside?"

He shook his head and held up his cigarette. "Mrs. Morrison don't allow no smoking inside. That's why I'm out here instead of inside still cleaning up the tractor from yesterday."

I stood hipshot, my hands jammed in my back pockets. "Okay with me. Just tell me what you know about Emmett Patterson. What he did, what kind of person he was, and anything you remember about yesterday."

"I already told the cops."

"Good. That means you won't have to think that much when you tell me."

He frowned at me. "Huh?"

"Look, I know you've told your story once. I even told Mrs. Morrison this investigation was a waste of time, but she insisted. And you know how she can be when she insists." I rolled my eyes, a male nuance that suggested *we're in the same boat with the old lady.*

The scowl on his bulldog face broke into a conspiratorial grin. "Yeah. She can be tough. A lot of things are tough," he added cryptically. He took a deep drag and blew the smoke out through his nostrils, a trick that always choked me when I smoked.

"Well, there ain't much to tell. Ain't you going to take notes?"

"I got a good memory, Mr. Runnels."

With a shrug, he continued. "I didn't like the guy. He was a punk. Lazy, always trying to dodge work. I never understood why Lonny kept him on."

"Lonny?"

"Yeah. Lonny Jackson, our Master Distiller, Emeritus. Alonzo Lynch Jackson. He's . . ." Runnels hesitated when he saw me arch an eyebrow at the ostentatious title. He grinned crookedly. "I ain't sure just what that emeritus business means, but that's what Mrs. Morrison wants him called. Seems like those big distilleries in Tennessee and Kentucky call them head honchos that emeritus thing."

I shrugged. Only in America.

He continued. "But, Lonny Jackson is a fair man . . . most of the time. I've seen him dump guys for a lot less than Emmett Patterson done . . . or I should say, didn't do."

"Got any ideas why he put up with Patterson?"

Runnels studied the question a moment. "Naw. Ask him."

"How long had Patterson worked here?"

"Ten years or so, I think. Let's see." He squinted his eyes and wrinkled his forehead as if the facial contortions would force the old memories from his brain. "He came here about the time the girl disappeared. Yeah, maybe a little after. No, it was before."

A bell went off in my head. "Girl? What girl?"

Runnels shrugged and lit another cigarette, a menthol. "Way back, a runaway girl passed through. Nice little girl. I didn't know she was a runaway then, but when she turned up missing a while later, the cops come by. Don't know if they ever found her or not. But Emmett, he was here then because I remember him flirting with the girl."

"Oh." For a moment, I thought I might be on to something, but the bell stopped clanging. "What about yesterday? You see him?"

"Not until the tractor ran over him."

"You saw the tractor run over him?"

He shrugged. "Not exactly. When I stepped outside, the tractor was going past the tree, and there wasn't no one driving. I didn't see nothing else for a few seconds, and then this dark pile sort of squirted out from the discs."

I grimaced at his picturesque description. "Then what?"

"Not much. I didn't pay no attention. Then Mrs. Morrison showed up. She waved me over."

I glanced at the tree. "What was his main job around here?"

Runnels shook his head. "No main job. Besides me and Lonny and the lab people, everyone here is a kind of jack-of-all-trades."

"You mean, everyone drives the tractors, forklifts, and so on?"

"Yeah. That was Emmett. Just manual labor. He didn't have the smarts for the laboratory. They do quality control stuff in there. Some of them even taste the whiskey."

Sounded like my kind of work. I wondered how much I would have to pay them for the job, but I dismissed the idea. Probably had all the tasters they needed anyway.

I looked around the distillery grounds. Behind the maintenance barn was a row of cottages, all of the same Spanish facade as the distillery and the main house. Each had a chimney and a stack of firewood next to the door, just as the distillery itself, which was set in the midst of a grove of oaks at least a hundred and fifty years old. My eyes focused on the one under which Emmett was killed.

A shiver ran up my spine. "Some operation you got here. You take care of all the equipment?" I nodded to the trucks, forklifts, tractors, and farm implements lined up in the maintenance barn. I eyed the logo, a white circle, in the center of which were the red letters CHD, joined in such a manner to form what looked like a backward D connected to a forward D by a horizontal bar. Reminded me of a barbell.

"Yeah. What with the maintenance on the distillery, it takes all my time."

"This is a lot of equipment for one person to take care of. You responsible for all of it?"

Runnels' crumpled face lit. "Every last bit. And none of

it ever stays outside. That's why it lasts so long. Why, the old lady, she'd fire my rear end if I didn't treat the equipment like a good looking woman."

I chuckled at his analogy. "Looks like you do a good job." I was serious.

With an air of surprising conviviality, he replied, "Hey, thanks. I appreciate them words. Of course, I get some help from time to time." He took a last drag on his cigarette and flipped it in an arc through the air. "Any more questions, Mr. Boudreaux? I got work to do."

"Yeah. One more. Who took out the tractor yesterday?"

"Hawkins. That's another punk. Him and Emmett run together. All these kids today are punks."

"How come Patterson ended up driving it?"

Runnels shrugged. "Beats me. That all?"

"Yeah. Thanks."

He turned to the barn, then hesitated and looked back at me. "You think Emmett was an accident?"

His question surprised me. He was the second to ask that question. "What do you think?"

He shrugged. "Beats me. I ain't talked to nobody about it." He glanced furtively around the grounds. He ignored my question. "You talking to everyone?"

"Everyone who worked with Patterson. Cleyhorn gave me a list. No sense in talking to those who had nothing to do with him. At least, at this point. Maybe later. Why? Don't you think it was an accident?"

Once again, he ignored my question. "Talk to Hawkins. He threatened to kill Emmett one time. And be sure and don't forget Mary Tucker. She oughta be on the list. If . . . anyone . . ." He clamped his lips shut. "Well, I ain't saying no more. Just talk to both of them. You hear? Of course, Mary ain't here today. Didn't show up for work. Wasn't here yesterday either. At least, no one saw her if she was. Mighta been on another bender." He sneaked a glance over his shoulder.

I tried to finesse him. "Why do you think they're so important?"

That didn't work either. He shrugged. "I ain't saying it wasn't no accident. In fact, I ain't saying no more. Just you be careful. Only last week, I spotted some of them hiding behind the cabins where our employees live. By the time I got there, they was gone."

I leaned forward, feeling my pulse speed up. Maybe I was on to something. "They? Who?"

Finally he answered one of my questions. "Aliens. I escaped from them, and they've been trying to take me back up."

Back in the pickup, I pulled out my notebook to jot down the information I had garnered from David Runnels. I hesitated. What information had I picked up from him? Christ, he was a delusional nut running around hiding from aliens. How could I believe anything he said? Still, I put down as much detail as I could remember.

When I finished, I glanced over the notes. Not much, but I learned early on that detailed notes from several witnesses sometimes dovetailed with each other. Like a puzzle. And who could say? Maybe Runnels' fanciful flights into Never Never Land might fit in somewhere.

But, I doubted it.

Chapter Four

My next stop was the distillery disguised as a Spanish hacienda. I paused outside the door and picked up a piece of firewood that had fallen off the pile. "My good deed for today," I muttered, tossing the log back on the stack.

Inside, the huge building was as spotless as an operating room. I looked around for a receptionist. A flight of stairs on one wall led to offices above.

The only information I spotted was a sign pointing up the stairs with MASTER DISTILLER, EMERITUS engraved in neat black block letters, in a style like they used in Arab countries.

I paused halfway up the stairs to gaze out over the distillery below. The building seemed a mile long, filled with the oddest collection of equipment I had ever seen, a mélange of stainless steel tubs and pots, each large enough to hold three eighteen wheelers parked side by side. Workers in long white lab coats scurried about.

At the top of the stairs was a door with a square glass pane. Above the door was another engraved sign: MASTER DISTILLER, EMERITUS. I looked inside at the man behind the desk. So that was a Master Distiller, Emeritus. I don't know what I expected. Probably a pot-bellied little man dressed in a Bavarian costume with a jaunty cap, and carrying a stein of beer. Instead, I saw a neatly attired businessman in an expensive three-piece suit poring over sheaths of data. The gray at his temples gave him the look of distinction, of wisdom, of breeding. So much so that the small Band Aid on his cheek looked out of place.

A welcome smile erased the seriousness on his thin face when he spotted me. He waved me in, quickly coming around the desk and offering me his hand. I guessed him to be a little over six feet, maybe six-two, about four inches taller than me. A slight man, his tone was soft and somewhat reticent, as if he was unsure of each word. "Mrs. Morrison said you were coming. I'm anxious to help in any way I can." He dragged the tip of his tongue over his lips. "Like everyone else, I want to see this tragedy behind us, and, if you'll pardon my saying it, forgotten about. Scandal plays havoc with stock prices." A sheepish grin replaced his warm smile.

"Seems like I've heard that before."

His cheeks colored. Quickly, he apologized. "I'm not a cold person, Mr. Boudreaux. Believe me. But, I've been here over thirty years. Chalk Hills Distillery is my life, my child you might say . . . at least, that's what my wife and daughters claim at times." He grinned shyly and added, "Every new batch I bring out is an attempt to create a sour mash bourbon superior to that of the previous run."

"I understand, Mr. Jackson." I threw out a piece of sardonic humor. "After all. Money makes the world go round."

He took me seriously. "Absolutely, Mr. Boudreaux. Absolutely."

I hesitated, my gaze flicking momentarily to the Band Aid on his cheek.

He caught my look. "Excuse the dressing. Cut myself shaving this morning."

I chuckled. "I've been there." It must have been some cut to warrant a Band Aid. I usually just stuck a piece of tissue paper on one, but then, I don't have emeritus printed after my name. Maybe you bleed more with such a title.

I glanced about the office. The second-floor window was

shaded from the morning sun by the ancient oak under which Emmett had been found.

"Now, what can I do for you, Mr. Boudreaux?"

"All I'd like to do is ask a few questions, and then I'll get out of your hair, Mr. Jackson."

"Go right ahead. I'll tell you whatever I can about Emmett or the distillery." He paused. "Have you ever toured our facility, Mr. Boudreaux?"

"No."

His eyes lit with an excited glitter. "You've missed quite a treat then."

With a shrug, I replied, "Every man to his own poison. I prefer drinking bourbon than watching it boil and bubble."

He wagged his finger at me. "Not bourbon, Mr. Boudreaux. Sour mash bourbon."

"There's a difference?" I frowned. "I thought bourbon was bourbon, like vodka is vodka."

"Oh, no. Bourbon comes from Bourbon County, Kentucky. All the other bourbons must be called sour mash. By law. Just like champagne comes from the province of Champagne in France. Elsewhere, it is considered sparkling water, although that propriety is not observed in America with the same fastidiousness as bourbon."

I gave him a wry grin. "Live and learn."

"Yes. And now, come with me." With a surprisingly powerful grip, he took my elbow and turned me around. His entire personality became electric, intense, a diametric switch from his earlier reserve. "I'll answer all your questions, Mr. Boudreaux, all of them, but you must permit me to show you through our plant and then join me in the visitors' lounge. I'm quite proud of the operation. And I think after you see it, you will enjoy your libation even more."

Before I could say no, hold on, or maybe next time, he had me downstairs in front of a display case containing hundreds of empty whiskey bottles of every size and color. "I always start here, with my collection. And this one, I think you'll appreciate. Circa, 1840. I like to show this one to all our guests," he said, pointing to a brown bottle shaped like an eighteenth century cabin with a door, windows, and chimney. The brand on the bottle was EG BOOZ'S OLD CABIN WHISKEY. "If the occasion should ever arise, Mr. Boudreaux, there is the origin of the word 'booze'."

I chuckled. "So EG Booz was the real McCoy, huh?"

He laughed. "Another whiskey first, Mr. Boudreaux."

"Huh?" I frowned.

"Real McCoy, Mr. Boudreaux. Real McCoy. The expression came from Captain Bill McCoy, who quite skillfully and successfully smuggled whiskey into the USA during Prohibition."

"No kidding?" Trivia fascinated me.

He gave me a condescending grin. "No kidding. That is the origin of that expression, Real McCoy. During Prohibition, unscrupulous gangsters paid no attention to the quality of the product they merchandised. As you are no doubt aware, a number of people died from bad whiskey. Everyone knew, however, that if they purchased whiskey from Bill McCoy, it was safe, and usually of the highest quality. Patrons would ask the bartender if the drink was the McCoy."

Then, he pointed through a window. "Now, back to business. Here is where the grain is unloaded and the corn, rye, and barley are placed in their respective bins prior to being ground."

I had to admit, it was quite an operation. I realized I wasn't getting away without seeing the entire plant, so I was determined to get in my share of questions.

He continued his explanation of the various operations in the distillery. He pointed out the grinding mills, huge machines shaped like upside-down U's. He spoke with the staccato beat of a machine gun. It was almost like he had some obsessive-compulsive disposition where the distillery was concerned.

I struggled to squeeze a word in edgewise. "I didn't see you out at the accident yesterday."

He pointed out where the various grains were stored after grinding. "Now, this . . . huh? Oh, no. I wasn't outside. I was upstairs, checking chemists' reports. I glanced out the window and saw a small crowd, but I had no idea what had happened."

I remembered catching a glimpse of a face in the second-floor window. It must have been Jackson's. "So, you went on back to work?"

He gave me an embarrassed grin. "Like I said, I didn't know what had happened. All I saw was a group of people. And in all truth, I'm not too comfortable in crowds, but I did attend the reception. In fact, I saw you with Mrs. Morrison's grandniece. Why . . ."

I slipped another question in. "But you knew Emmett Patterson pretty well."

For a moment at the mash tubs, he paused. I saw a flicker of something in his eyes, nervousness, impatience. "In all candor, too well. I didn't like the man. He was a lazy and slipshod employee." He gestured to the cookers, quickly shifting the subject. "Here is where the corn is cooked to two hundred and twelve degrees. Then we cool it to one hundred and eighty, add the rye and cook it again. That's how we make the mash. Once the mash is cooled to one hundred and forty-five degrees, we add the malted barley. Now, up ahead is the yeast laboratory. You'll be amazed at what we have accomplished. Why . . ."

His words faded as I glanced out the window at a black Lexus passing, each tire stirring up tiny puffs of white dust. "Why didn't you fire him if he was such a poor employee?"

He reached for the doorknob and without hesitation, replied, "This is a business, Mr. Boudreaux. We all have supervision."

I followed him into the lab, surprised at the sterility of the room, but curious as to the obvious implication of his remark. "You're telling me Mrs. Morrison refused to let you fire him?"

He arched an eyebrow. "All I'm saying is that when I suggested we replace Patterson, my recommendation was rejected." He picked up a test tube. "Here's the amazing project I was talking about, a sample of our own strain of yeast which is cultured and protected from contamination and outside influences by careful bacteriological techniques. One of a kind, it is a pure culture yeast—Saccharomyces Cerevisiae—developed from a single original cell and carefully propagated and maintained until a vigorous strain was produced with its own particular properties to produce whiskey possessing desired characteristics. We made our first breakthrough in nineteen-eighty-eight, and we constantly strive to improve the yeast."

I was lost after *here is a sample of our own yeast.* "That's nice," I lamely replied, but I went right back to my earlier question. "Why would she refuse to let you fire him?"

His voice fell back into its initial reticence. "She signs my pay check, which is quite substantial. Her business is her business. Mine is mine. I don't argue with her." He gave me a crooked grin. "I can't afford to, especially with a wonderful wife and two lovely, but spoiled daughters accustomed to the good life."

"I see."

Immediately, that obsessive-compulsive mindset took charge again. "Now, the next step is the fermenting room where yeast is added to mash and allowed to ferment for up to ninety-six hours."

He spat out explanations and observations like a ruptured fire hose as we toured the fermenting room. The fermenters were huge cylindrical vats almost forty feet tall and twenty in diameter. The bottom was shaped like a funnel, and pipes ran from the fermenters in every direction, reminding me of one of those old Rube Goldberg contraptions. You've seen them—a steel ball rolls down a groove, falls off on a lever that ignites a cigarette lighter, which in turn burns a string in two, upsetting a bucket of water on someone's head.

"This is really something." I didn't know what else to say. Jackson was like a child in a toy shop. I supposed that if someone was ever born to be a Master Distiller, Emeritus, it was Alonzo Lynch Jackson. I managed to squeeze in another observation. "Your mechanic, Runnels, suggested maybe someone killed Patterson."

Jackson looked around in surprise, then a wry grin creased his face. He touched his tongue to his lips again. "David is an excellent mechanic, but sometimes he . . . well, the most generous observation is that sometimes his imagination runs away with him." He led the way past the beer wells and into the room with the copper whiskey stills. "Did he tell you about his friends from another planet?"

I sensed the gentle sarcasm in his words. "So you think the death was simply an accident?"

"Yes, Mr. Boudreaux." He smiled almost compassionately. "A tragic accident. Of course, Emmett helped it along by getting drunk, but, that was Emmett."

"Drunk? How do you know that? The autopsy report hasn't been released."

He grinned sheepishly. "Not to speak badly of the dead, but Emmett was drunk. That was what caused the accident. Now, shall we continue our tour? At the end, we can sample some of our latest sour mash bourbons."

Well, I perked up at that. After all, I was gaining an invaluable education in one area of my nutritional needs, even if my investigation was leading me nowhere, which is exactly what I had expected. "Sounds like a winner to me."

In the next hour, he pointed out the whiskey condenser, the wine tanks, the finished whiskey tanks, and then led me into the cistern room where finished whiskey was being drawn off into new, charred white oak barrels. I watched as workers stenciled black numbers on a white rectangle on each barrel with the type of whiskey, the date, and a number."

I read one of the numbers. "Four-nine-eight-two-one-two-eight. Why the number?"

Jackson grimaced. "Serial numbers. Uncle Sam. He's got to have his part of this."

"You mean, every barrel is numbered?"

"Every barrel. Like that one you just read. It will be stored in rackhouse number four. The ninety-eight is the year barreled, and the barrel number is two thousand, one hundred and twenty-eight." He nodded to a computer next to a file cabinet. "Here's where we keep record of our inventory. And there," he said, indicating the file cabinet, "is where we keep our old records on floppy disks going back to the early eighties. Before that, we kept our records by hand."

"And every single one of those barrels, you have records on?"

He handed me a printout. "A necessity, Mr. Boudreaux. The federal government insists on exact records. They want to know just how much taxes you're going to pay. That printout gives the type of whiskey, the date, serial number, and rackhouse location."

"Rackhouse?"

"A warehouse of sorts. That's where the whiskey ages."

I nodded. "Where do you store all these barrels? Here on the premises?"

"Not enough room. We have three rackhouses on the premises and several more around the area. The barrels are white oak, charred inside. Each holds one hundred and eighty liters of whiskey, which ages for up to twelve years."

"How much do you produce a year?"

Alonzo Jackson grinned shyly. "We're not a world player yet, Mr. Boudreaux. Just a little over one hundred and twenty thousand last year."

"Gallons or liters?"

His grin broadened. "Barrels."

"Some operation," I muttered as we left the cistern room and headed across the quadrangle for the lounge. I noticed a long, low, rectangular building adjoining the distillery. "What's that?"

He snapped his fingers and angled toward the building. "I'm sorry. I should have thought to show you that piece of history. It is fascinating. It's where the Saladin Box is."

"The Saladin Box?"

He opened the door and flipped on the lights. The room was empty, obviously closed up for years as evidenced by the accumulation of dust clinging to every exposed surface. In the middle of the floor was a concrete trough with a perforated floor. The trough was eight feet wide, four feet deep, and at least eighty feet long, the length of the building. Extending the length of the trough were six mechanical turners that resembled giant, flat-bladed corkscrews.

"What's this contraption?"

With a chuckle, he led the way along the bay. "This contraption was once used to turn the barley, slowly moving it from one end of the trough to the other." He went on to explain that barley had to be turned and dried properly for good bourbon. "However, the box was too labor intensive, so now we buy the barley from specified vendors."

"How much barley are you talking about? Very much?"

"The box holds about twenty tons of barley, which will make about sixteen or seventeen tons of malt."

This whiskey business was more complicated than it looked. "I'd hate to turn that much by hand."

Alonzo arched a gray-flecked eyebrow. "That's exactly what Tom Seldes did in the beginning . . . before the Saladin Box. His main job was to start at one end of the building, which had a foot thick layer of barley covering the entire floor, and work his way from one end of the room to the other, turning all of the barley by hand, day in and day out."

I remembered Seldes, the gorilla man. No wonder his arms and shoulders looked so powerful. "Twenty tons? What did he use?"

"A shovel, but that was years ago. Certainly he wasn't turning twenty tons then. More like ten or twelve."

"That's all?" I gave him a wry grin.

Alonza nodded. "That's all."

I whistled. "That's enough. I suppose he's been around a long time, huh?"

"Yes. He started with Mr. Morrison in the beginning. Through all the bad times, and finally the good times. Tom and Mr. Morrison were great friends. In fact, that was the reason the Saladin Box was put in."

"What do you mean by that?"

"Tom developed what is called monkey shoulders in the business. Years and years of the constant turning of barley creates a muscular condition that was the precursor of repetitive strain injury. Similar, I would guess, to the current affliction called carpal tunnel syndrome, except this, obviously, is in the shoulders."

I looked at him in disbelief. "You're telling me that Morrison went to all of this expense for one man?"

Jackson laughed. "Oh, no. Primarily, we did it because business had grown so that hand turning was not cost effective. Then soon, the Saladin Box also became a victim of the economy. As I mentioned earlier, now we can purchase sufficient grains meeting our specifications from various vendors."

At the end of the tour, he led me into the visitors' lounge, which perpetuated the Spanish motif of the distillery. A dozen heavy oaken tables, their chairs upholstered with rich red velvet, filled the room like tiny islands, each a discreet distance from the others. Red and black tile, shiny and slick, formed a series of diamonds on the floor. Oils in dark, ornate frames covered the stucco walls, scenes of violent bullfights, dancing *senoritas,* and whirling *fandangos*. I was especially drawn to an oil of a dauntless *vaquero* leaning low off a galloping horse, arm outstretched, his extended fingers ready to seize the neck of a rooster partially buried in the sand.

Jackson gestured to a table. I sat, noticing a current copy of the *Austin Business Report* on the table. I glanced around the room. Each table had a copy of the magazine, which was, as its title implied, a monthly report on thriving businesses in and around Austin.

No sooner had we seated ourselves than a fruit plate and

platter of deli sandwiches were set before us. Jackson nodded to the waiter. "Thank you, Fred." He spoke to me.
"Now for the bourbon. Any special requests?" Like magic,
Alonzo Jackson's conversation mode leapfrogged from
obsessive-compulsive back to reticent and shy.

I popped a watermelon ball in my mouth. "Whatever you
say."

For the next few minutes, we made small talk about the
distillery until Fred brought us each a mint julep, the drink
of the Old South. I've never been partial to mixed drinks,
being of the opinion that mixers, whether water or soda,
only delayed the goal and intent of serious drinkers.

But, I was in polite society that would frown on my
turning up the bottle and chugging half-a-dozen gulps. So
I sipped daintily of my drink. A woman's drink, I told
myself. Then I remembered the missing girl. "Were you
here when the girl turned up missing?"

He momentarily stiffened, and then a frown wrinkled his
forehead. "Missing girl? Oh, that one. Yes, yes. I was
here."

"What was it all about?"

"Why? Is it related to Patterson in any way?"

I shook my head. "Just idle conversation. Runnels mentioned her."

The wrinkles faded from his forehead. "Oh. I don't remember too much. Transient. She was passing through and
stopped for a job. I sent her to Tom at the rackhouse. He
had a full crew, so the girl left. A few weeks later, the
police showed up. I gathered from the way the police talked
that the girl was a runaway from some backwoods town in
Tennessee. Just as well he didn't hire her. I don't think she
was interested in the whiskey business." He sipped his julep
and licked his lips. "A true classic drink, Mr. Boudreaux.
True classic."

"What do you mean, 'not interested in the whiskey business?'"

He shrugged. "The way she was dressed. A white blouse
knotted at her midriff. Shorts pulled right up into her

crotch. I prefer employees who dress appropriately. That demonstrates they do indeed want to work here, to help us produce superior sour mash bourbon." He gestured to the fruit tray. "Please, help yourself."

There was a trace of arrogance in his words that irritated me. "She might have worked out real well."

He grinned sheepishly at the testy edge on my words. "I sound pompous, I know. Please, forgive me, but, first impressions, Mr. Boudreaux. First impressions. Personally, I think she was more interested in finding a young man than working. I didn't want to take a chance. Just the short time she was here, she was the cause of an argument between David Runnels and Emmett Patterson. I didn't witness the trouble, but from what I heard, blows were almost struck." He gestured to the fruit and sandwiches. "Please. Help yourself."

The next few minutes were passed in innocuous chitchat. After four watermelon balls, two tiny triangles of cantaloupes, one strawberry, and four cream cheese and ham sandwich quarters—which were so small they would not even sustain a Barbie doll—I finished my second drink and excused myself. Alonzo Jackson offered his hand, thanked me and, ordering a third Mint Julep, leaned back in his chair, the picture of an old southern gentleman relaxing on the verandah after a hard day of working his slaves.

Chapter Five

I paused just outside the door and blinked at the bright Texas sun, then glanced at my watch.

"Son of—" I muttered. I'd spent almost four hours with Jackson, and other than his reinforcing Runnels' opinion of the deceased as well as my own of Runnels, I learned nothing. "Maybe, it's like you told Morrison, Tony. You can't learn anything when there is nothing to learn," I muttered, squinting through the rising heat rays that contorted the landscape into garbled visions.

I looked around the grounds. The main house, its bright red roof tiles contrasting sharply with the white stucco walls in the bright sun, showed no sign of life. The large doors remained open in the maintenance barn, and I could see David Runnels busy at work.

Checking my notebook, I decided to see if Mary Tucker had shown up. I was curious as to just what it was about her that seemed so disturbing to Runnels.

Halfway across the lot to the maintenance barn, a white Mercedes convertible with two laughing young women slid to a halt several feet away. Dust ballooned up around the car.

The passenger, her white teeth a striking contrast to her deeply tanned skin, motioned to me. "Hey, you there. You seen our dad?"

The driver was a couple of years older, but that they were sisters was obvious. "I don't know. Who's your dad?"

She frowned. "You work here?"

"Not quite."

She studied me a moment, then her smile popped back on her face. "Alonzo Jackson. He wasn't in his office. One of the lab technicians said he was showing some dude around."

I arched an eyebrow, then gave them a easy grin. "Well, I'm the dude, and your dad is over at the visitors' lounge. You know where that is?"

"Naturally." She laughed and waved as the Mercedes sped away.

I watched them a moment, shaking my head. I had the feeling they went through money faster than politicians change their promises. No wonder Jackson never argued with Beatrice Morrison. He couldn't afford to lose his job.

I found Runnels in the barn replacing a battery in a fork-lift.

"Naw. Tucker never punched in." Runnels stuck a crescent wrench in his hip pocket. He dragged a stained handkerchief from his pocket and wiped his face.

I glanced at the cabins. A rusty Chevrolet Cavalier sat in front of one, and an electric-blue Camaro in front of another. "She live in one of those?"

"Yeah. Number five, but she ain't there. Been gone all night, I guess."

"Oh?"

"Car's gone. Drives a red Honda. Front left fender is all boogered up." He jammed the handkerchief back in his pocket. "You wantin' to talk to her, huh?"

"Tomorrow will do just as well."

"She hangs out at the Red Grasshopper on Sixth Street in Austin."

I made a throwaway gesture with my hand. "I'll see her tomorrow."

He gave me a crooked grin. "She's got bright red hair if

you change your mind. Goes with the Honda." He laughed
at his own wit.

"Thanks. I won't. By the way, Jackson said you and
Emmett had words over that runaway girl you mentioned
earlier."

His bulldog face darkened. "Yeah. Emmett was trying to
get in her pants. I told him I'd bust his head if he did."

"Did he?"

Runnels' eyes hardened. "Yeah. At least, that's what I
heard."

"And did you? Bust his head, I mean."

He sighed. "No."

I studied him a few moments, then nodded. "Thanks, Mr.
Runnels. And thanks for the information about Mary
Tucker."

I didn't plan on looking up Mary Tucker, not right away.
Instead, I swung by the Travis County Forensics lab where
an old girlfriend worked. Carrie Jean Adams, Landry now.
She and I had both been teachers at Madison High School.
She taught biology for a couple of years, but the struggle
with spoiled children, snotty parents, and stingy school
boards finally drove her into the laid-back, good-old-boy
security of county government, which also paid much better, was less of a hassle, and easier on the nervous system.

Carrie Jean's desk sat beside an opaque glass door, in
the middle of which was the word LAB in two-inch gold
leaf that was flaking away.

Eight desks filled the remainder of the room, four on
either side of the aisle leading to the door. Five women sat
staring at their computers, faces intent with concentration,
fingers flashing as they inputted data. The unmistakable
scent of eau d' formaldehyde, accented with the none-too-
delicate pungency of pine oil, floated about the office. I
wondered idly if any of the women's husband's or boyfriend's pheromones were stimulated by the smell on their
ladies' clothing.

Florescent lights recessed in the white tile ceiling gave the room a bright newness that somehow seemed incompatible with the mission of the office, that of processing the dead. Black curtains, shadows, and candles perched crookedly on the computer monitors was the atmosphere I had expected, not this.

Carrie Jean's face lit when she spotted me. She hurried to me and pressed her cheek to mine in a politically correct gesture of friendship. She'd put on a few pounds, but that's married life. She still looked good.

Back at her desk, I lowered my voice and told her what I needed.

"I shouldn't, Tony." She gave me a come hither glance, knowing full well I wouldn't come hither because she was married to my college roommate who stole her away from me.

"Hey, what can they do? You're a supervisor. Thirteen years on the job. Who would even know? You handle the paperwork anyway. Just make an extra copy."

Her voice grew husky. "What's in it for me?"

I played her game. "What do you want?"

"You don't want to know. You'd freak out."

"Try me."

She hesitated, the taunting, teasing grin fading from her face. She couldn't decide if I was calling her bluff or not. She laughed nervously and, lowering her voice, quickly changed the subject. "Okay. Who do you want?"

I lowered my voice at her sudden caution. "Emmett Patterson." I glanced over my shoulder, then back to Carrie.

Her eyes met mine, then her gaze dropped to the folder on the side of her desk.

"Is that it?"

She nodded.

I reached for the folder, but she laid her hand on mine. "I'll make you a copy. How do I get it to you?"

"I'll meet you after work. Where are you parked?"

"North parking lot. Green Accord. Five-fifteen."

* * *

On the way out, I checked the time. Three forty-five. If I hurried, I could check out the Red Grasshopper on Sixth Street and get back by five-fifteen.

I always swore Sixth Street in downtown Austin modeled itself after New Orleans' Bourbon Street. The seven or eight-block stretch from I-35 to downtown was lined with cozy little bistros, clamorous dance halls, expensive brothels disguised as bars, and a variety of eating joints selling everything from fried ants to Italian-styled fajitas.

At four o'clock in the afternoon, pedestrian traffic was no greater than any other of the downtown streets, but come seven o'clock, the sidewalks erupted into a mass of reveling, frolicking merrymakers jamming the streets and making heroic efforts to guzzle every can of Millers Lite or Budweiser in the city.

Runnels had steered me right. I spotted the red Honda, boogered up left fender and all, parked just down the street from the Red Grasshopper. I found a parking spot around the corner.

There were half a dozen tables in the room, all filled, but Mary Tucker stuck out like a boil on a baby's backside. I spotted her as soon as I pushed through the doors. Her red hair was frowsy, her makeup thick and gaudy, and her tight pink tube top cut her fleshy torso in two, compressing her ample bosom into the shape of a squashed pillow, providing no definition at all for her breasts. She sat at a rear table with three men who looked like they'd stepped out of the old black and white Victor Mature movie, *One Million BC*. Empty beer bottles stood on the table like a clan of grunting Neanderthals leering at a woolly mammoth roasting over the fire.

I took a stool at the bar and ordered a draft beer. The room had the usual warm, sweet smell of beer, tinged with the sharp odor of alcohol. My kind of perfume. I took a deep breath. If I'd lived in the old West, I would have been either a professional gambler or a bartender.

The four were laughing and shouting, obviously drunk. The three men leaned forward, eyes glittering, each imagining the nectar of Mary Tucker's debatable favors. For a moment, I hesitated. I was staring at trouble ready to explode. Maybe I should wait until tomorrow. I sipped my beer, and a tiny flame of irritation licked at my temper. Why wait? All I wanted was five minutes of her time.

Beer in hand, I slid off the barstool. As one, the four looked up when I stopped at the table. The eyes of the three men narrowed, but the shine in their eyes was unmistakable. The nervous rapping of knuckles on the table, and the stupefying euphoria emanating from the group confirmed my suspicions. Whether they were kissing Mary Jane or bouncing goof balls, I couldn't guess, but whatever they were toking, they were amped sky high. I spoke quickly. "Mary Tucker? My name is Tony Boudreaux. Mrs. Morrison asked me to visit with you for just a few moments."

I glanced at the men for their reaction, then I continued. "There was an accident at the distillery, and she hired me to speak with all the employees. Do you have a few minutes? I won't take long."

One of the men, a burly gorilla wearing a black tank top, pushed to his feet. Tattoos and curly hair covered his flabby arms and rounded shoulders. His belly stuck out like a basketball. He growled at me. "Beat it, buddy. We was here first." Then he belched.

Wisdom suggesting discretion in this case, I held up a hand. "Not cutting in, friend. In fact, I'll buy you boys a round for three minutes of conversation with Ms. Tucker here."

A second man, long greasy hair and sunken face, sneered. "Ms. Tucker. Jeez. Who you kiddin', man?"

Mary Tucker's face turned as red as her hair. "Shut your mouth, you slob." Her words slapped the thin man in the face. She gave me a gap-toothed grin, then glared back at the chastened boyfriend. "That's how you're supposed to talk to a lady. You could learn some manners."

He glared up at me.

I gave her, and me, an out. "Tomorrow at the distillery will do, but since we're here, I figured to save some time."

The third man, of average build, about fifty, just stared at me with the coldest pair of black eyes I'd ever seen.

I spoke directly to him. "What do you say, friend? A round of beers for a couple minutes."

"You're a narc."

Greasy Hair stiffened. Tattoo Arms reached for his hip pocket.

Chapter Six

 The bar grew silent. I felt every eye focus on me. I forced a laugh. "Yeah. A narc. You bet. And you're Tom Cruise."

A low chuckle from around the room eased the tension. The other two numbnuts hesitated and turned to my accuser, who kept his eyes fixed on my face. He sneered. "So you say."

"Look, friend. All I want to do is talk to Mary about an accident at the distillery. That's it, then I'm outta here."

Mary Tucker dug her long, red nails in Tattoo Arms' shoulders and jerked him back into his seat. "Sit down, Rue." She glared at the other two. "Both of you shut up. I wanta hear about this accident." She turned her watery eyes on mine. "What happened?"

I looked at her friends, then cut my eyes back to her. "Can we talk in private?"

She sneered at her admirers. "You heard. Go play some music or something."

I tossed a ten on the table. "My treat."

Tattoo Arms snorted. "Keep your money."

Grumbling, the three rose and staggered to the bar, throwing baleful looks over their shoulders at me. I'd made some enemies.

"Now, what happened, buster?" Mary Tucker turned up

her beer and promptly poured some down the front of her pink tube top. She slapped at her breasts. "Crap. Waste of good beer." She gave her chin and throat a couple of cursory wipes, then gulped down the rest of her beer noisily. She sat the mug on the table and daintily stifled a belch.

I located the rear exit, then took a chair facing her companions. I set my half-full mug of beer on the table. "Emmett Patterson is dead. Run over by a tractor."

Her puffy face went blank. I could see my words registering in her eyes. A satisfied grin slowly curled her red lips. "When?"

"Yesterday morning."

"Heaven be praised. I wish I'd been there to see him. I hope that no-good died hard."

I pictured the scene in my mind. Steak tartare. "Yes, ma'am. I think I can truly say he died hard."

She slurred her words. "So what does the old lady want from me?"

"Just tell me what you know about Emmett. That's all. This is just routine, Mary. I'm talking to all the employees."

Her eyes narrowed. "You think I killed him?"

"No. Like I said, I'm talking to all the employees. That's all. It was an accident."

With a grunt, she leaned back in her chair. A blubbery roll of white flesh appeared from under her tube top. "He was slime. I'm glad he's dead. I just wish I'd had the guts to kill him myself."

I glanced at her friends who were eyeing me warily. They reminded me of snarling Rottweilers straining at the leash. "What did he do to you?"

Drunkenly, she jerked her head around and blinked her eyes, trying to focus on me. "What did he do to me? I'll tell you what that no-good creep did to me. He knocked up my girl, that's what he did. He put the screws to everybody. He was the lowest form of scum."

Her eyes filled with tears. Before I could reply, she continued, the words spilling out faster than beer out of a mug.

"My little girl was eighteen, and he sweet-talked her into his bed." She hesitated, then drew a deep breath and barged on, her voice growing louder. "Her and me talked about it when she found out she was pregnant. We was going to keep the baby, you know. We figured her and the kid could live at the distillery with me. I'd work. We'd make it okay, but Emmett and her had a fight, and she fell. Miscarried. Tore up her female parts, the doctor said."

Mary Tucker paused, tears cutting deep channels through the thick orange makeup on her face. "She never can have no kids no more." A sob caught in her throat, and a tear and her thick mascara started to run.

"Where is she now?"

Mary's bottom lip quivered. She dropped her chin to her fleshy breasts. "I dunno. I come in from work one day, and she was gone. The note said she had to go out and find herself." Her shoulders shook, and she wagged her head from side to side. "Find herself. Ain't that a load of crud? Poor kid. Ain't heard nothing in five years." More tears rolled down her cheeks. "Far as I know, she's dead."

I glanced around. Everyone in the bar was watching. From the corner of my eye, I saw her companions easing toward us. They saw the tears, and in their besotted brains, there was only one person to blame. I handed her a handkerchief. "Here, Mary." I glanced at the three hulking brutes edging closer and closer. I was growing antsy. "You'll mess up your makeup, Mary. Now, you don't want to cry, do you? Huh? Do you?" I glanced anxiously at the approaching Neanderthals.

She nodded, and with a whining sob that could be heard all over the Red Grasshopper, she dropped her head in her arms and wailed like a baby.

Maintaining my composure and struggling to be very professional and matter-of-fact, I rose, nodded to the shaking shoulders, and said, "Thanks for your time, Mary. You've answered all my questions."

I turned to the front door, but Tattoo Arms stood in my way. "What did you do to her, buddy?"

The other two glared at me. The quintessence of innocence, I said, "She told me about her daughter. Has she told you guys about her daughter?" I stepped back and gestured to the table. "The last thing she said to me was that since you four were such good friends, she wanted you to have a chair so she could tell you about her daughter."

They eyed me suspiciously. All the while, Mary Tucker sobbed and moaned, from time to time breaking into a screeching, ululating wail that would have shamed every police cruiser in Austin.

Greasy Hair pulled his hand from his pocket. On his fist, he wore a set of brass knuckles the size of Alabama. "Looks to me like you done hurt her, mister."

"Yeah," Tattoo Arms grunted.

Like I said, I'm no Sherlock Holmes, but even a bozo with the IQ of a refrigerator bulb could see those three simians were ready to rearrange every attachment on my body. You know, stick my arms where my legs should be, and vice versa. I forced a laugh. "Hey, boys. You don't understand." I reached for my beer and toasted them. "Let me explain."

Abruptly, I kicked a chair into Greasy Hair's knees and threw the beer in Tattoo Arms' face. The third goon dived across the table at me. I jumped back and slammed the mug down on the back of his head. I leaped for the rear exit and raced down a narrow hall lined with stacks of beer boxes, which I yanked as I passed, spilling them on the floor behind me. Ahead, the back door beckoned.

I slammed through the screen and hit the alley behind the Red Grasshopper in full stride, sprinting toward the street. The curses and shouts behind me grew louder. I slid around the corner of the alley and almost ran into a Jesus freak garbed in a gray robe and carrying a cross down the middle of the sidewalk.

I vaulted in my truck. Never had I been so glad to hear that engine roar to life.

Just as I pulled away from the curb, Tattoo Arms,

followed closely by his cohorts, burst from the alley and slammed into the Jesus freak, sending them all sprawling to the sidewalk in a tangle of arms, legs, and wooden cross.

The afternoon traffic was murder. In fact, traffic just about anytime in Austin was murder. With typical Texas logic, Austinites have decided that I-35 makes a more convenient main street than Main Street. The drive to the forensics lab took twice as long.

Carrie Jean was waiting in her green Accord, engine running, windows up, and air conditioning on high. She rolled down her window when I pulled up beside her and, without a word, handed me a manila envelope.

"Thanks." I winked at her. "I owe you."

She arched an eyebrow seductively, nodded, and drove away.

I watched as she turned onto Lamar Boulevard and sped away, trying to imagine what our life together would have been like. All single people ponder that question from time to time, but I'd been there once, split the sheets, and in the process, learned enough to recognize the fact that I did not possess the degree of commitment marriage demanded. "We might have made a year," I muttered, knowing full well that I wasn't willing to share my life with anyone just now.

Commitment. That was another reason my relationship with Janice Coffman-Morrison had stalled. I just wasn't willing to put out the effort. Macho pride was another. She was rich. I was too hardheaded to be a kept man. Embedded deep in my psyche by generations of Boudreauxs, all the way from Nova Scotia to Church Point, Louisiana, resided the deep conviction that a man took care of his family. The man, not the woman. "We wouldn't make even a year," I muttered as I pulled the Chevy into gear and headed for my place.

Besides, before I settled down, I had a couple of goals; one to prove my old man wrong wherever the heck he was.

The other was to be rich. The former, I could handle; the latter, a dream.

The apartment was dark, the blinds drawn. Jack lay on the couch, a rag on his forehead, a moan on his lips. I shook my head. "You still alive?"

"Barely."

I knew the ravages of hangovers, and like most men, took a perverted delight in taunting the unfortunate soul who suffered one. But, at the moment, I was more interested in the file on Emmett Patterson than making Jack's life miserable. I turned the light on in the kitchen and opened the envelope.

"Bless your heart," I muttered to Carrie Jean as a sheath of copied documents slid out.

I flipped through the report, searching for the death certificate. "Here we go," I whispered, holding the document so the light could catch it. Quickly, I found line thirty-five, part one. Immediate cause of death. Exsanguination. The deletion of blood. I arched an eyebrow. No argument there. All the blood had certainly been deleted from his body.

The next line was the secondary cause of death. Multiple lacerations. I arched a second eyebrow. No argument there either. At least, it sounded more professional than *chopped to bits*.

The next line gave the coroner's explanation of the death: Farming accident. The only evidence of residual drugs in his system was an alcohol level of .21/mgL. I shook my head in wonder. Over twice the level of legal intoxication. Halfway to the toxic level of .4. Maybe he did just pass out. He was drunk enough.

"What do you have there?"

I looked up as Jack staggered in, his bloodshot eyes sunk in deep holes. "Nothing. Just some reports."

"Oh." He shuffled to the sink and filled a glass with water. "Oh, man, I wish I could die."

"You look like you did."

He tried to muster a grin, but failed miserably. He shuffled back to his dark refuge.

I spent the next several minutes reading and rereading the file. *After transflecting the scalp and piecing the fractured skull together, a blunt trauma to the occipital region was located.* "Probably where he hit the back of his head when he fell on the frame of the tandem discs," I muttered, wincing at the horror the poor guy must have experienced in those last few seconds of his life.

My eyes came to an abrupt halt when I reached the list of his personal belongings: Alden chukka boots; a Rolex President, 18 karats, quartz; two diamond rings. Quickly I reread the list and whistled.

How could a distillery worker, probably making no more than eight, ten bucks an hour afford that kind of luxury? A Rolex President had to be twelve, fourteen thousand. And I had a hunch the diamonds were real, not the diamoniques most people buy from QVC today. Anyone who wears a Rolex isn't likely to wear fake diamonds. Then there were the chukkas. Aldens. You couldn't get Alden chukkas for less than four hundred, unless you stole them from some guy's locker.

All of a sudden, I had the feeling I might be looking at a piece of work that could very well stretch the definition of accidental death. I'm not one of those PIs whose brain operates with the intuitive leaps and bounds that always seem to reveal staggering perceptions. I stumble forward, one plodding step at a time, but this time, I saw my next step with amazing clarity. Find out how Emmett Patterson afforded the luxury of a six-figure income on laborer's wages.

A tiny flame of excitement ignited in my chest. Maybe there was something more to this case, something no one knew about, or no one would admit.

Digging my notes from my shirt pocket, I read back over them, trying to make pieces of the puzzle fit. Suddenly, I hesitated, rereading my notes from the maintenance supervisor, David Runnels. He said Hawkins had taken the tractor out Sunday morning, yet at the scene, Hawkins told Sergeant Ben Howard that all the tractor work had been completed. Then why would he take out the tractor if all the job had been finished?

I glanced at the clock. Not yet six-thirty. On impulse, I decided to drive back out to Chalk Hills Distillery. Maybe I could catch Claude Hawkins, and while I was there, interview Tom Seldes, the rackhouse foreman.

Just as I stepped on my porch, I hesitated. A black Lexus pulled away from the curb across the street. Its windows were tinted, making it impossible to see who was driving. I watched the vehicle disappear around the corner. I remembered the black Lexus I'd spotted out at the distillery during my tour of the facility with Jackson. Could it be the same one?

"Jeez, Tony," I muttered, discarding the idea even as I climbed in my truck. "There's probably only ten thousand black Lexus cars in Austin."

What I didn't find out until later was that as soon as I pulled out and headed for the distillery, the black Lexus fell in behind me.

Chapter Seven

The sun hovered just above the oak-covered hills to the west by the time I reached Chalk Hills. Evening shadows stretched their first fingers across the distillery. Lights shone from the maintenance barn. I spotted Runnels leaning into the engine compartment of a red Ford pickup. One thing about the man, he worked late.

Mary Tucker's red Honda, boogered up left front fender and all, was parked in front of cottage number five. The battered car seemed to sprawl out, like a worn-out red-tick hound. Her place showed no sign of life. Either she was resting up from her two-day party, or she had brought it with her.

There were four other cottages, the lights on in two. When I spotted the electric-blue Camaro in front of one of the darkened cabins, I whistled. I had failed to notice earlier, but the car was a Yenko, complete with white stripe, chrome rally wheels, and no doubt a monster 427 lurking beneath the hood. Somehow, I sensed it belonged to the dead man.

I pulled up beside the rusted hulk of an old Chevy Cavalier in front of number three. I got lucky. Hawkins answered my knock. When he saw me, he grinned crookedly and shoved the screen open. "Wondered when you would get here. Come on in. Beer in the fridge if you don't mind Old Milwaukee."

I grinned back. "My favorite."

The cottage was two rooms—one the bath, the other everything else. A worn carpet covered the concrete floor. In the back corner beyond the door to the bath sat a mattress and box springs. No headboard. In the other rear corner was the kitchen area, a metal table, one-piece cabinet with sink, a chipped and wheezing refrigerator, and a two-burner apartment stove. The front half of the room contained a sagging couch, two threadbare recliners, and a brand new fifty-two-inch color TV that had the honor of sitting on the fireplace hearth.

The entire affair was decorated in contemporary baseball. A gun rack hung on the wall, but instead of shotguns or rifles, it held three baseball bats, the barrel of one appearing to be of a lighter color than the handle. Almost as if it had been deliberately bleached.

"Nice decor," I said, easing carefully into one of the recliners, hoping a spring didn't unspring and jab my butt.

He plopped on the couch and muted the sound on the TV. He gestured to the collection of baseball memorabilia cluttering his walls. "Yeah. I'm a baseball nut. Play on a local softball team." He paused, tossed his head to sling his greasy hair from his face. "Well, what do you want to know?"

"Same thing I asked the others. Tell me what you know about Emmett Patterson."

"Besides the fact I still hate the jerk even if he is dead?"

I studied the lanky man facing me, his long hair stringing down over his shoulders. One thing about this guy, I told myself, he comes straight to the point. "Even if you hate him, Claude. Do you mind if I call you, Claude, Claude?"

He snickered. "Just Claude. Not Claude Claude."

Oh, Christ, I thought, now I got me a standup comic. "Right. So, what do you know about Patterson . . . Claude?"

"Not much more than anyone else, I suppose. We partied together. I'll say this about the dude. He could party. Girls always liked to see him show up because he partied longer than anyone else, and spent money like it was going out of style. That's his Camaro sitting out there. Man, the chicks loved that car."

My instincts had been right. The Camaro was Patterson's. I chuckled and tossed out what I hoped would be a provocative observation. "He must've won the lottery or something."

Hawkins just frowned. "Huh?"

So much for provocative observations. "I mean, he wore expensive clothes and watches. He drove a Yenko Camaro. If he spent like you say, he had to have a money source other than the distillery here."

The lanky man's face twisted in concentration, obviously a most difficult task for him, and evidently, one he seldom attempted. "Yeah. You know, I never thought about that, but now that you bring it up, old Emmett did have money to burn, except when it came to paying me back. In fact, that jerk is the reason I'm driving that bucket of rust outside. I lost my nineteen-ninety-six Silverado pickup back to the finance company because of him."

I stilled the surge of excitement bouncing up and down in my stomach. I gave him a sympathetic frown. "Oh?"

Hawkins pursed his lips. "Yeah. Emmett owes me over six hundred bucks." He hesitated, shrugged. "Well, hey, he owed me. Don't figure I can collect from a stiff, huh?"

"Who knows? Probably with the right lawyer."

He laughed. "Yeah. Hey, man, you hear the joke about the lawyer and the shark?"

Last thing I needed was to get strung out with a good old boy and his jokes. "Yeah. That was a good one, wasn't it? Now, what about the money? The six hundred dollars?"

The frown of disappointment faded from his face. "Oh, yeah. Well, we had words last week. I owed the finance company two months on my pickup. Emmett claimed he didn't have the cash. I told him I was going to kick his tail if he didn't get it."

"Is that when you told him you were going to kill him?"

His cheeks colored. He ducked his head. "You talked to Runnels, huh?"

I arched an eyebrow.

He shrugged. "Yeah, but I was just running off at the mouth, man. Honest."

"Did he get you the money?"

"Naw. He come begging me for a little more time. Said there was no way he could get the cash until the end of the month. I slapped the snot out of him, and he started bawling like a baby." He paused and gulped down several swallows of his beer. Sheepishly, he added, "I couldn't hurt nobody. Truth is, I felt sorry for the whining creep, even if he was into me for six big ones. Anyway, finance company took the Silverado, and I ended up with that piece of junk out there."

"Sounds like the guy was a real winner," I remarked, my tone heavy with sarcasm.

Hawkins shook his head. "Huh? Oh, no, man. He wasn't no winner. The guy was a loser."

For a moment, I stared at him. Then I cautioned myself to limit my conversation with Claude to simple, direct words. No insinuations, no implications. I had the feeling he was down to his last few hundred brain cells.

"Yesterday, you told Sergeant Howard that you weren't scheduled to work except to clean up after the reception."

He nodded and leaned back on the couch, propping his feet on the coffee table. "So?"

"Well, I'm sure it was a misunderstanding, but Runnels said you took out the tractor yesterday. Why would you do that if there was no work to do?"

"He's full of it. I didn't take no tractor out. Either Emmett or Tom did. I think I saw Tom on it yesterday morning."

"Tom?"

"Yeah. Tom Seldes, the rackhouse foreman. He lives next door."

I jotted in my notebook. Like the puzzled remark Alice uttered on her trip through Wonderland, things were getting

curiouser and curiouser. "So, you didn't take out the tractor?"

"Nope. Hey, old Runnels is wacky. Between him and
those aliens he claims are hiding all over the place, you
never know what to expect."

"Why would anyone take the tractor out? Everything was
already disked."

He gave me a lopsided grin. "My question exactly."

"You said you saw Tom Seldes on it?"

He screwed up his face. "Yeah. I think I saw him on it.
Truth is, I never paid much attention. I saw somebody, but
I ain't sure who. He might not have been the one."

"Say Tom Seldes was on the tractor. Any reason for him
to have it out?"

"Not that I know of. Like you said, the disking was
done."

I glanced back over my notes for any other questions I
wanted to ask. "So Emmett was a ladies' man, huh?"

Hawkins grinned, revealing a set of yellow teeth with
some kind of unidentifiable fungus growing between them.
"Man, as much as I hate the creep now for stiffing me, I
got to admit he sure was one for the ladies. And good
lookers, no old ones who sagged. He liked them young and
firm. He was fast, too, man. Why, way back, some girl
come through. Hitchhiker." He leered. "Never forget her.
She wore a red shirt that showed her belly. Her pants pulled
up tight." He shook his head and blew through his lips.
"She was sure a looker. She hadn't been here ten minutes
before old Emmett had her out in back of rackhouse number two. That's how fast he was. Just about the time they
finished, old Tom, Tom Seldes . . . you know, the one we
was talking about."

"Yeah. Go on."

"Well, old Tom walked up on them. According to Emmett, him and the girl finished up while old Tom stood
there watching, his mouth hanging open."

"What happened then?"

He wrinkled his thin face in concentration. "Seems like

she went over to the lab then, but I ain't sure." A lazy grin popped back on his face. "Anything else?"

I shrugged. "No. Not really. What'd you do after the cops left?"

"You mean yesterday?"

I wanted to roll my eyes, but I remained professional. "Yes. You know, after they took Emmett away."

He gave me a sheepish grin. "Crashed. I was drunker'n a skunk. That's why I don't remember much. I slept 'til old Tom woke me to clean up after the reception."

"You talk to anyone about Emmett?"

He frowned. "You mean yesterday?"

"Yeah. Yesterday."

"Naw. Except when the cops was there. Me and Tom talked about it later when we was cleaning up. That was all."

I was out of questions. I pushed myself to my feet. "Hey. Appreciate your time."

Claude winked. A happy grin leaped to his lips. "Anytime, man. Anytime. Glad to help."

When I left Hawkins' cabin, I noticed the lights were off in Tom Seldes' place. I decided to let him wait until tomorrow. Besides, I needed some time to go over my notes. As usual, some contradictions had popped up, such as the color of the missing girl's blouse. Jackson claimed it was white; Hawkins said red. And no one knew exactly who took the tractor from the garage.

I had an uneasy feeling that the words "accidental death" on the death certificate might be subject to a re-evaluation. All of a sudden, a few curious holes were appearing in the accident theory.

I wasn't trying to build a murder case, but the fact was just about everyone I interviewed had a reason to kill Emmett Patterson. Mary Tucker most of all, because Emmett got her daughter pregnant and caused the miscarriage. Hawkins was next in my book because of money. Then Runnels, because Emmett was a punk, which wasn't much of a reason for murder, although given the right set of circumstances, it was more than sufficient.

Last came Alonzo Jackson, the Master Distiller, Emeritus, who simply and unequivocally, disliked the man.

I grunted. Good thing it was an accident. If it had been murder, there was a handful of people who could step to the front of the line.

Hey, as far as I knew, maybe the aliens whacked the guy.

The lights were still on in the maintenance barn, so I pulled up and went inside. A morbid curiosity impelled me to take a closer look at the tractor and discs that had done the job on Patterson.

The brightly lit barn was so large that five high school gymnasiums could have fit inside, a sad indictment of the expensive accouterments of business versus those of education. On the other hand, it was cleaner than my apartment, an ironic indictment of gainful labor versus sloth and indifference.

The company vehicles, trucks, pickups, and farm implements shone like they had just been given a coat of wax. I had to admit, Runnels took good care of the equipment. I glanced around. He was nowhere to be seen. I circled the tractor and cringed when I imagined Emmett falling off the seat, straight down in the path of the circular blades.

I paused at the rear of the tractor and stared up at the seat. That's where he had been sitting. According to Sergeant Howard, the tractor bounced over the ditch, causing the drunken Patterson to fall from the seat.

I crossed the room to the discs and tried to figure out just where he might have struck the frame, suffering the blow that knocked him unconscious. I ran my hand over the heavy frame, a sturdy web of square steel bars supporting the X-shaped rows of discs. I stared at the huge implement, and at the same time I had the strangest feeling I had just forgotten the punchline for a joke.

"Find what you're looking for?"

I jerked around. David Runnels stood staring at me, his bulldog face showing no expression. "Nope. Just looking. Hope you don't mind. I'd been over talking to Claude Hawkins and saw the lights on in here. I just wanted a closeup look at what killed Emmett." I glanced at the discs. I rubbed the back of my neck as the feeling I was missing something swept over me again. But what?

Runnels bristled. "Don't blame my machines. Emmett killed Emmett. Around dangerous tools, a man's got to be careful. He wasn't. No one's fault but Emmett's." He turned to the door. "I'm shutting down for the night. Anything else?"

Reluctantly, I turned away from the discs. "No, thanks. See you later."

He grunted.

"Oh, hey. Yeah. One question."

"What?" Runnels pursed his lips and knit his heavy brows. "What question?"

"Hawkins claims he didn't take the tractor out yesterday. I probably misunderstood, but I thought you said he did."

Runnels stared at me as if he had no idea who I was. "Huh?"

"Yeah. Hawkins says he didn't take the tractor out."

His eyes narrowed, and his nostrils flared. "You calling me a liar?"

His burst of anger surprised me. "No. Just telling you what I was told."

My explanation seemed to mollify him.

I wanted to drop the issue to keep from irritating the man again. Guys with alien connections unnerve me, but I had to know the truth. "Was he lying to me, Mr. Runnels?"

He snorted. "I don't know. You best check with old Tom."

"Seldes? Why?"

"He's the one what told me Hawkins took out the tractor."

Another puncture in the accident theory. "I see. Sure." I

waved and stepped back. "I'll see him tomorrow. Good night."

He grunted.

I grunted back.

During the drive back to my apartment, I went back over the events of the day. The day? It seemed like I'd been on this case a month. I always talked aloud to myself about my cases while I drove, a habit that more than once brought puzzled glances from other drivers, who figured they had just spotted some manic-schizoid asking himself questions and then gleefully answering them.

But the process worked for me. I guess you could say I was more of an audio learner. Connections came easier for me by hearing than reading. All through college, I read assignments aloud. Drove my roommate, Harold Landry, nuts. Maybe that's why the sneaky cretin stole Carrie Jean away from me. Revenge, although he probably came out on the short end.

So, there I was, driving down the dark, narrow road with the distant lights of Austin lighting the bellies of a bank of slow moving clouds, jabbering away to myself and blinking at the set of bright lights following me. Too close.

I came up with a few questions for which I wanted some answers. Patterson's expensive tastes, for one. Where did the money come from? The truth about who took out the tractor, for another. And whatever was nagging me about the discs, for a third.

And finally, I muttered to myself, glaring in the rearview mirror, I wanted to know why the bozo in the car behind was tailgating me. That's how Bubba picks a fight in Texas, by tailgating. I swung onto the shoulder and slammed on the brakes.

I jumped out of the pickup and, tire tool in hand, stomped back to the black car that pulled up behind me. As usual, I would pattern my behavior on the size of the person who climbed out of the vehicle. I could be mean, or I could be charming.

I caught my breath and jerked to a halt as the stand-in for Godzilla unfolded from the luxury car.

"Charming" was the word of the day.

Chapter Eight

Godzilla's double was so enormous, he didn't walk. He lumbered. I stood motionless in the glare of the headlights, the tire tool burning a hole in my hand. I decided now was the appropriate time to employ my charm. I gently eased the tire tool out of sight behind my back and side-stepped to get away from the glare of the headlights. "Anything wrong?" It was a deferential statement that wouldn't irritate anyone, I hoped. "You were following mighty close."

The guy had to be seven feet tall, but his bulk was counterpointed by his hand-tailored suit, which I could tell was expensive even in the light of the headlights. I had no idea what brand, but it wasn't Sears. He paused, looked down at me like a T-Rex measuring how far he would have to bob his head to snap up his next meal. From the peripheral glare of the headlights, I made out a square face that looked like a chunk of chipped granite—square, solid, with no distinguishing features other than a couple of fissures for eyes, a square knob for a nose, and a third crevice that was probably his mouth.

He came right to the point. "Mr. O'Banion wants you should come see him." He spoke in a measured rumble without a trace of inflection.

I glanced at the car. A Lexus. I remembered the black vehicle at the distillery, then later, outside my apartment.

"O'Banion? Danny O'Banion?" Which was a stupid question because I only knew one O'Banion.

Godzilla nodded.

Danny O'Banion was Austin's resident mobster. That was the talk, although nothing had ever been pinned on Danny. No one really knew his ties or connections. There was a lot of talk, a lot of speculation about the Mafia, Cosa Nostra, the Chinese Triad, the Mexican Mafia. At local bars, bordellos, game rooms, it was O'Banion this, O'Banion that. As far as I knew, all talk. Nothing else.

But Danny and I had a history, back in the eleventh grade when we scrambled through a few scrapes together. Then Danny left school before his senior year. Naturally, we drifted apart, but those months during our junior year bonded us. I ran into him at one of the annual football games between my alma mater, UT, and Oklahoma up in Dallas one year. We hit each other on the shoulder, lied a little, sipped from his silver flask a lot, and then went our separate ways.

"Where is he?"

Godzilla pointed his finger at me. It was the size of a link of sausage. "You follow me."

"Lead on, McDuff." I turned back to my pickup, but a huge hand grabbed my shoulder and turned me back around. I felt like my shoulder was caught in a vise. I would have sworn I heard the rotor in my shoulder shatter.

"My name ain't McDuff. They call me Huey."

I held up my free hand in a gesture of apology. "Sorry. Huey. I meant, you go. Me follow."

He grunted and released my shoulder. He climbed in the Lexus.

Huey led me over a couple of back roads before turning onto another highway that led to Lake Travis. Danny's abrupt appearance puzzled me. What did he have in mind? A class reunion? I doubted that very seriously. He wouldn't have had Huey tailing me for the last twenty-four hours just to announce a gala get-together. The only other reason had to be the death of Emmett Patterson. And that made even less sense.

Traffic was typical for a Monday night, miles and miles of Texans jammed bumper to bumper, speeding up, slowing down, darting in and out, pushing the seventy-mile-per-hour speed limit to eighty.

The mindset of Texas drivers is to follow as closely as possible, and regardless of speed, never leave enough room for another vehicle to slip into, or they will. And finally, with the cold resolve of a western gunfighter, Texas drivers abhor turn signals, believing there is no sense in giving the guy behind some clue as to your next move.

Huey must not have been a native-born Texan for the right blinker on the Lexus flashed, and the black vehicle turned onto a narrow, one-lane road that wound up one of the hills overlooking Lake Travis. Ahead, car lights flashed. I looked around, searching for a house, for anything, but all I saw was a forest of stunted oak and cedar growing out of chalky-white limestone. A perfect spot for a kiss on the lips.

The brake lights of the Lexus lit the night with a red glare as Huey stopped just past the parked car, obviously intending for me to stop beside the vehicle at the side of the road.

I braked to a halt and rolled down my window. Danny O'Banion grinned up at me from the window of his car. "Long time since Dallas, Tony."

"Ten years, Danny." I glanced around the dark countryside. Below us, the highway looked like two strings of Christmas lights, all white. "I sort of figured on a fancier place for our reunion than out here in the middle of nowhere."

He laughed, that same old infectious Danny O'Banion laugh that had a disarming charm on everyone. "Sorry, but I need the privacy."

"For what? This isn't where I get my kiss on the lips, is

it?" I was clearly puzzled as to the reason for such a clandestine meeting.

He chuckled. "You watch too many movies. No, it's about the guy at the distillery who got himself killed." Before I could reply, Danny continued. "Look, Tony. It's a long story, and I'm not going to bore you with it. I know the old lady hired you to investigate it. To come up with independent proof that it was an accident. Bottom line for me—was it an accident?"

I studied the cherubic face looking up at me from the other vehicle. I suppressed a rush of irritation. "Come on, Danny. What's it to you?"

His grin faded. "Just say I'm curious."

"No." I shook my head. "You pulled me out here with no explanation. You want to know if Patterson's death was an accident. Be realistic. For you to go to all this trouble, it has to be something besides mere curiosity."

"Yeah." He chuckled. "Look, I don't blame you for wondering, but honest, old friend, I got my reasons. They're another whole story. You wouldn't be interested."

Which was a polite way of telling me to stick my nose somewhere else, which also brought up another question. Just what was Danny O'Banion's involvement with the distillery?

He continued. "A favor, Tony. That's all I'm asking."

As usual, his irrepressible charm swayed me. He was the sort you couldn't help liking, that little boy demeanor. "What the heck. You just want to know if it was an accident or not?"

"Yeah."

"It looks that way, Danny. I'm sure there are probably some around who had reason to kill the guy, but all the hard evidence points to an accident." I did my best to give him the bare bones of the police report. My suspicions, I kept to myself. "It appears he got soused, took a joy ride on the tractor. When he went under the tree, he ducked, the tractor hit the ditch, and he bounced out. It was that simple. Satisfy you?"

Danny studied me. "Yeah. But do me another favor. You find out any different, let me know. First off." He hesitated.

"I don't understand, Danny. Now, what's this business to you? You owe me some kind of explanation."

His grin faded. "I'm looking into it for some business associates."

Business associates? I frowned. His kind of business associates, I didn't want to mess with. "Sure. Why not?"

Danny hesitated, studying me. Maybe he felt he owed me an explanation after all. "Thanks. Hey, look, we go way back. All I can tell you is I'm involved with some influential people who have sizable investments out there as a result of a contact I provided. These are people who want to keep a low profile."

His voice dropped lower. "These are gentlemen you or a bozo like me don't want to make mad. If there's a murder, and their involvement becomes public, my friends will be very upset with me. That would blow my credibility all the way to China, and me right along with it. You understand?"

I considered his explanation. Influential people could mean mob members, and despite their efforts to curry the image of legitimacy, those good old boys weren't too inclined to take the same risks as legitimate investors. If that's what he meant, and if I were in his shoes, I'd be nervous too. "I don't want to know nothing. But I understand." I grinned. "How can I get in touch with you? We can't keep meeting out here. People will talk."

"Huey'll be around. Just look for the black Lexus."

I grunted. "Just knowing Huey'll be around makes my day."

Danny chuckled. "I bet." He leaned back and the window hissed shut. The powerful automobile sped away, heading for the string of Christmas lights on the highway below.

I watched until the lights were swallowed up in the line of headlights. Shifting my truck into gear, I turned around and headed home, puzzling over Danny's involvement with Chalk Hills. One thing I knew for sure, I didn't want to get on the wrong side of his 'business associates.'

And now, in addition to all the unanswered questions I had uncovered at Chalk Hills, Danny O'Banion had stepped into the snarl, further tangling whatever few threads of coherent logic remained.

Jack lay on the couch, snoring and gurgling. Oscar swam lazily in his aquarium, having survived another day with the infamous Barb and Angelfish killer, Jack Edney. I watched the pale pink Tiger Barb for several moments, weaving through the plastic water sprite and Amazon sword plants.

"I know how you feel, guy," I whispered, sprinkling some food on the surface. "Around and around. Getting nowhere."

My stomach growled. The refrigerator was empty, so, after showering, I sat at the snack bar, eating a bowl of frosted flakes and rereading the file on Emmett Patterson. The pieces of the puzzle refused to fit.

At three o'clock in the morning, I bolted upright in bed. I suddenly realized what had been bothering me about the set of tandem discs, and I knew without a doubt, Emmett Patterson had been murdered.

Chapter Nine

I stared into the darkness, unable to believe the revelation that had exploded in my head. But, it made sense. After reading the autopsy report and interviewing most of those involved, I had the feeling I was stumbling across uneven ground, marked by potholes and yawning chasms. But now, with a single stroke of startling recognition, the entire playing field leveled off.

Eagerly, I threw back the covers and hurried into the kitchen, ignoring Jack's dissonant snoring reverberating off the walls. With trembling fingers, I flipped through the autopsy report to the descriptions of the trauma. "Here it is," I muttered, reading aloud the words that told me Emmett Patterson had been murdered. "A blunt trauma to the occipital region. It other words, a concave, non-penetrating wound to the back of the head."

I held the death certificate in both hands, my fingers gripping the edges until they crumpled. "That's it. That's what I was missing. Blunt trauma to the occipital region."

Which was impossible.

The frame supporting the discs was angular, made up of square bars with ninety-degree corners, sharp corners. Had he struck the frame, the trauma would have been penetrating, not blunt.

And if the wound did not match the frame of the tandem

disc, then perhaps he did not pass out and fall from the tractor. Unless someone had helped him pass out with a club of some sort, a round club. I thought of Claude and of a round baseball bat, the round baseball bat with the bleached barrel. Maybe bleached to remove the blood stains?

I was too excited to sleep. I wanted action; I wanted to wade into the fray and find answers to the entire set of new questions tumbling in my head. But three-thirty in the morning is too early for anyone to ask questions, even those out at the distillery. Still, by the time I shaved, grabbed breakfast at IHOP, and reached Chalk Hills, the early birds would be after the worms out there.

And that was my job. To find the worm who murdered Emmett Patterson.

I hesitated, considering the other side of the sword. If it was murder, Beatrice Morrison and Danny O'Banion would be upset, and that's putting it mildly. They'd go ballistic. "You best be sure, Tony," I muttered, folding the autopsy report back into the envelope. "Dead-on sure."

I jerked to a halt on the porch. I should have known. Baby Huey sat in the Lexus next to the curb across the street. A cigarette glowed. I considered inviting him to IHOP. "Let him pay for his own," I muttered, pulling onto the street and heading west. Moments later, a pair of headlights swung in behind me.

Huey sat in the Lexus while I had a leisurely breakfast loaded with cholesterol and fat. Three eggs over-easy, three greasy sausages, two pancakes dripping with butter and hot blueberry syrup, all washed down with hot coffee heavily laden with sugar. Carbohydrates, fat, protein. A balanced breakfast. I could feel my arteries clog. To offset the year's worth of fat and cholesterol coursing through my veins after such a meal, I sipped on a diet Coke during the drive out to Chalk Hills.

* * *

I'm not too swift, but my next decision was a no-brainer. If I learned for certain that Patterson was murdered, then I had to turn it over to the proper authorities. But first, I would inform Beatrice Morrison and Danny O'Banion. Once each decided on his next move, then I would go to Sergeant Howard and dump the details in his lap without fear of learning to swim with concrete shoes.

However, until I followed up on my theory, I would keep my suspicions to myself.

The only employee I had not interviewed was Tom Seldes, the rackhouse foreman, the heavily muscled man with gorilla arms and girl's voice, the man whose personal ambiance still jarred me. No way a brutish man should have the voice of a bird. He should growl, like a gorilla.

He stood in the middle of the sunlight spilling through the open doors of the rackhouse. Behind him, barrels of aging whiskey were stacked in horizontal racks four high, on rows that stretched into the darkness of the storage building.

He wore khaki trousers and a matching shirt, unbuttoned at the neck. Thick, black hair boiled from his open collar. We shook hands. His grip was like a vise.

Though friendly, Seldes was not the least bit helpful. Pulling information from him was like dodging raindrops, almost impossible. "You knew Emmett Patterson pretty well, didn't you?"

"Yeah," he said in his high-pitched voice. "Emmett was okay. He hadn't grown up altogether, but he was a good boy." He shook his head. "Terrible way to go."

"How do you think it happened?"

Seldes arched an eyebrow. "Beats me. Claude said Emmett was drunk."

"You talk to anyone else about it?"

"Naw. The others, they don't mess much with us common laborers out here. Of course, don't misunderstand. They're good folk. But we don't run in the same circles."

Before I could reply, a bright red forklift rounded the

corner of the rackhouse and headed for us. "Best we move out of the way," he said, stepping to the side of the open doors. "The boys will be pretty busy today."

"Doing what? They moving barrels?"

He rolled his powerful shoulders. "Some of them." He looked up at me, his dark eyes bright. "I been in this business for over fifty years. Still fascinates me."

Dodging forklifts? The stench of diesel? The chill of a darkened rackhouse? Some fascination. "Yeah, I can see how it would be fascinating. Now, about Emmett Patterson."

Seldes shrugged. "Told you about all there is. He worked here for a long time. He knew better than to get careless on the tractor. That's how accidents happen. In fact, he shouldn't have even had it out Sunday. Especially drinking like he was."

A flag popped up in my brain. "Him? I thought Hawkins took it out."

"No. Emmett did."

"Maybe I'm confused. Runnels told me that you said Hawkins took the tractor out."

A wry grin split his deeply lined face. "David Runnels is a good man. I've knowed him for over thirty years, but he's losing it upstairs."

"You mean, Patterson took out the tractor."

"Yeah."

"Then why would Runnels say Hawkins did?"

His grin broadened. "Like I said, Mr. Boudreaux, David is at the age where he forgets a lot. He gets his days mixed up. I took it out Saturday morning. Emmett took it out Sunday morning."

Either Tom Seldes was a fast thinker and glib liar, or David Runnels had simply given me the wrong information. I didn't push the matter with Seldes. I'd verify the information myself. "Hawkins said Emmett was quite the ladies man."

The smile on his face turned into a frown. "I tried to get him to settle down, but he wouldn't listen. His lust for women kept him in trouble. His hormones was always going crazy."

"But according to Hawkins, he did have a knack to charm their pants off. Didn't you run across him and some girl in the rackhouse one time years back?"

His cheeks colored. "Yeah. I was plumb surprised. I didn't know what to do, so I just stood there like a dumbbell."

"That was the runaway girl?"

He nodded. "I don't know about a runaway, but she wanted a job, but I didn't want no truck with her. Hardheaded. She said Alonzo had sent her to me, and she insisted on filling out an application. I let her, but when I told her I didn't need any help, she got mad. Wanted to go back and talk to Alonzo about working in the lab." He snorted. "I didn't figure her and Emmett woulda got no work done at all. They'd jump in the nearest dark corner." He hesitated. "The girl had no shame at all."

"What do you mean?"

A sheepish grin played over his face. "When I found her and Emmett, she was wearing this red shirt that she got dirty when her and Emmett was . . . well, you know. Rolling around on the ground with Emmett. Anyway, she pulled that shirt off right in front of me and put on a white shirt before she went back to see Alonzo. And she wasn't wearing no brassiere neither."

I suppressed a smile at the obviously straitlaced man's discomfort over the girl's shameless behavior. "That must have been something of a shock, huh?"

"Yeah. I ain't no prude or nothing, but, well, right out in front of God and everybody, people don't strip off naked. You know?"

"Yeah." I hesitated, trying to figure out how I could get her name without arousing his curiosity. "Well, you know, Tom, Mrs. Morrison wants me to find out all I can about what happened to Emmett. I want to give her a full report. You know how she likes to get her money's worth. You wouldn't happen to have the girl's name would you?"

He knit his bushy brows, then shrugged. "Yeah. Her application is upstairs in the file cabinet, but that was over ten years ago. What good could she do?"

I gave him a conspiratorial grin. "Probably nothing, but you know how Mrs. Morrison is. As sure as I leave out someone, she'll want to know why. I figure if I talk to everyone, then she can't fault me for anything. Right?"

He pondered my reply. "I suppose. Though, it don't make a whole lot of sense to me. Ten years." He turned and headed up a flight of stairs. "Up here."

Maybe it was his physical features, the fact that he resembled a gorilla, bowed legs, long arms, that made me anticipate a cluttered office in chaotic disarray. To my surprise, the small nook above the rackhouse that served as his office was meticulously clean, judiciously arranged, and surprisingly orderly.

I stepped into the office and closed the door behind me while Seldes squatted easily and thumbed through a set of folders in the bottom drawer of his file cabinet. I couldn't help noticing the breadth of his shoulders and imagining the power in his arms. And what was more astounding was that the man had to be in his mid-sixties at least, maybe older. Yet, he had the build and agility of a thirty-year-old.

Throwing all those barrels around and shoveling all that barley, I guessed.

"Did Emmett work a second job?"

Seldes shook his head. "No." He straightened his back. "Here we are. Katherine Voss, Benchmark, Kentucky." He rose and handed me the application.

Quickly, I jotted down the pertinent data, address, father's name, telephone—that sort of thing. I glanced at the date: June 18, 1988. "I'm impressed, Mr. Seldes. This application is ten-years-old, and you went right to it."

"I like for things to be organized." He offered no other information or explanation, so I figured the interview was over.

"Thanks, Mr. Seldes. You've been helpful."

"Why did you ask about Emmett working on a second job?"

I folded my notebook into my shirt pocket. "He spent more than he made. Fancy clothes, fairly new car. And a Camaro like the one he drove doesn't come cheap. I'm trying to figure out how he did it."

At first I thought I imagined the slight stiffening of Seldes' body, but dismissed it as simply my imagination. Later, however, the more I thought about it, the more convinced I became that my remark had struck a nerve with Tom Seldes.

Sitting in my pickup, I gazed at Emmett Patterson's cabin as I ran back through my interview with Seldes. He believed the incident was accidental. At least, that's what he said. And that's how it appeared, except for the injury to the back of Emmett's skull.

On impulse, I drove across the parking lot and pulled in beside the Yenko Camaro. I wanted to look inside Patterson's cabin.

Making an effort to be casual just in case anyone was watching, I paused by the electric-blue vehicle, inspecting the Yenko racing stripe. I studied the vehicle, taking my time, giving the impression to whoever might be watching that I was carrying out the job for which I had been paid. It never ceases to amaze me just how far sheer gall will take a person.

I jotted a few scribbles in my notebook for the benefit of any hidden observer, slipped it back in my pocket, then casually tried the door to the cabin. It was unlocked. I stepped inside, deliberately leaving the door open. Same layout as Hawkins', except Emmett must have been a drugstore cowboy.

A set of six-foot horns adorned one wall, a ten-gallon hat on one tip, a baseball cap with the Chalk Hills Distillery logo on the other. Two pairs of alligator boots—one scuffed, the other shiny and polished with silver-tipped heels and toes—sat at the end of the bed, which was a facsimile of a cowboy's bunk. On the wall was a clock with a Lone Star face. On either side of the clock was an oaken plaque, each holding a Navy Colt ball and cap pistol, the muzzle of each facing the clock. Various pictures decorated the other walls; bucking broncs, a Charles Remington print, a Russell print, and a map of 1870 Texas.

Western shirts, bell-bottomed slacks, and two belts with buckles the size of washtubs hung in the closet. Next to the clothes chest sat a gun cabinet with glass doors. "What were you planning on doing, Emmett," I muttered, shaking my head at what I considered a fairly extensive collection of rifles and revolvers. I had to admit, he knew his guns.

My own collection is limited to a shotgun that belonged to my grandfather, and an airweight Colt Cobra, a snub-nosed .38 revolver with a bobbed hammer so it won't snag. And I certainly wouldn't call it a husky weapon. On a scale of one to ten, maybe a four, and that was a deliberate decision on my part. I don't want to get into situations that demanded heavy exchanges, and with the little .38, I was always somewhat more discreet in whomever I took on.

On the top of the clothes chest, a stack of crossword puzzle books lay next to a heavy ashtray heaped with assorted cartridges, 30-30s, .45s, .22s, 30.06s. I noticed some of the 30-30s had crosses cut in the slug, a simple trick to force the slug to expand upon impact. Now why would he want to do that? For the deer around the area? I picked up the slug to study it more closely. It slipped from my fingers and bounced off the concrete floor, then rolled under the gun cabinet.

I muttered a curse as I dropped to my knees and felt under the cabinet for the cartridge. I froze when my fingers touched a metal plate recessed in the concrete floor. I pressed my face against the floor in an effort to peer under the cabinet. "Damn," I muttered, glancing out the open door to see if anyone was coming.

Hurriedly, I slid one end of the gun cabinet away from the wall and stared down at a torch-cut metal plate set in the floor. I ran my fingers over the rough edges of the concrete around the plate, then using my fingernails, pulled the plate up.

I caught my breath. "Well, I'll be . . ." Beneath the plate was a safe with a combination lock. "Well, well, well. Now just what did you keep in here, Emmett?" I muttered to myself.

Even a pedestrian PI like me could tell that the safe had been installed after the original floor had been poured.

Gingerly, I touched the dial, pulling up on the remote possibility it might not be locked. Foolish dream. The vault at my bank couldn't be locked any tighter.

I glanced around the corner of the gun cabinet just as Claude Hawkins stepped through the door. He frowned. "Something wrong in here?"

"Huh?" Gripping the 30-30 cartridge tightly, I rose and casually pushed the cabinet against the wall. "Oh, no." I held the cartridge between my thumb and forefinger. "I dropped a slug, and naturally, it rolled under the cabinet."

He shrugged. "I was going to my place for a bite of lunch and saw the door open." He hesitated. "You talked to old Tom this morning?"

"Yeah." I dropped the cartridge in the ashtray and picked up one of the puzzle books. "Looks like Emmett was a crossword puzzle freak."

Hawkins nodded to the stacks of magazines and papers on the chest and then pointed to similar stacks next to the push-button telephone on the battered coffee table. "All kinds of puzzles. I never had no use for them, but he carried them in his hip pocket and worked them at breaks and lunch. He was a nut on puzzles. All kinds. You know, especially them that had three or four numbers and then asked what the next one was. You know the kind? Two-four-six. Now what comes next? He was always showing off about them. Me, I never could do any kind of puzzle," he added with a laugh.

I tossed the magazine on the chest, looked around the room, and headed for the door. "Me neither."

"You just about got your stuff finished?"

"Looks that way unless Mrs. Morrison wants me to do any more."

Claude stepped back outside. "What more is there?"

I gave him a crooked grin. "Who knows?"

He laughed. "Yeah. Who knows?"

Chapter Ten

I moved to Austin with my mother from Church Point, Louisiana when I was in the eleventh grade. That was twenty or so years ago, a few years after my old man left us. Mom and I liked it just fine in Austin, but she moved back to Church Point a few years later to take care of her ill sister. I remained.

Twenty-odd years is not long enough to build an extensive good-old-boy network that allows a first choice on box seats for the UT games in Darrel Royal Memorial Stadium. A *tour de force* of that magnitude is the result of a fifty-year network. My puny twenty-year network would get me end-zone tickets, and provide me with a few, not very influential contacts in various agencies. Luckily, some were in the right agencies, and unluckily, some were not.

Contrary to a lot of fiction, PIs are not the love children of the local cops. The native gendarmes take a dim view of anyone interfering with their investigations; consequently, you have as much chance leaping the Grand Canyon as taking a look at evidence they've compiled.

Unless.

Unless you have a friend who works in the Evidence Room of the local police department. Joe Ray Burrus transferred from UT to Sam Houston University at the end of his junior year, changing his major to criminal justice. We lost touch for six or seven years until we ran into each other at a boat show at the Convention Center in Austin.

Joe Ray was one of those free-thinking rebels who preferred staying just within the bounds of convention for the sake of comfort, the comfort of a steady paycheck. From time to time, depending upon how the proposition struck him, he pushed on the envelope, even on occasion kicking a hole in it.

"No problem," he replied with an impish grin at my request. "It's about time to stir up things down there. We haven't had any evidence stolen in two months."

"Hey, not steal. I just want to look."

"Like I say, no problem."

He was right. No problem.

I entered the side door of the police station, took the basement stairs instead of the lobby and, two minutes later, he stuck me at a table in a corner behind a dozen rows of shelves. On the scarred table lay a plastic bag and a pair of latex gloves. "Here's Patterson's belongings."

Even though I put on the gloves, I shuddered as I sorted through the torn and bloody clothing. I checked the brand of his chukka boot. Alden. Just like the report said. I looked for the Rolex President, but surprise, surprise. The Rolex had vanished along with the two diamond rings, probably accidentally flushed down the toilet or swept out with the trash. His wallet was hand-tooled leather, containing two credit cards, four gasoline stamps from Shamrock, no cash, naturally—which, just like the Rolex and diamonds, was accidentally lost—and several folded pieces of paper.

The papers contained nothing much, a few women's names and telephone numbers. One had a number which, at first, I figured was probably some account number: 1210841084284212.

Suddenly, my brain took one of those giant leaps into the realm of speculation. "I wonder," I muttered, considering the number. Why does anyone carry anything in a wallet? Because it has value, which meant this number had value. Obviously this one wasn't a telephone number, nor an address, nor a lottery number.

I chewed on my bottom lip. What could be so important about this set of figures that he carried it in his wallet?

The floor safe in his cabin flashed into my mind. My heart thudded in my chest. "Maybe it's the combination." With shaking hands, I quickly copied the sixteen numerals into my notebook, checking three times to make sure I had them in proper order. I paused. Maybe that giant leap had been too long. Whoever heard of a combination with sixteen numbers? I knew nothing about combination locks. I did know that the safe had been added after the cabin was built. That being the situation, he probably could have had any combination he wanted put in.

Maybe.

My initial enthusiasm somewhat dampened by realistic skepticism, I copied his social security number and, from his checkbook, his bank account number. According to the check register, which was only three weeks old, he had made a five-hundred-dollar deposit two weeks earlier. The register showed no balances. I tore out a blank check and slipped it into my shirt pocket with my notebook.

At the nearest Southwestern Bell carrel, I dialed his bank. Finding the balance was a snap. I had his most recent deposit and social security number. I listened in disbelief as the bookkeeper informed me Patterson's balance was six thousand, two hundred, and thirty-one dollars. Oh, and a few odd cents.

I whistled, staring at the receiver in shock. Six grand. I thought of Claude and the six hundred Patterson had stiffed him for. I grunted. "Emmett, you cheap little creep." Still, where did he get the money? He had told Claude he couldn't put his hands on any until the end of the month.

Either Patterson moonlighted, which he didn't, or he was thrift personified, which he wasn't, or he provided a stud service for rich, old ladies, which he wouldn't, or—or what? What was another option? The lottery? Dream on.

Inheritance? No way. Drugs? Other than alcohol, none showed up in the autopsy. Of course, some dealers never touched the stuff.

My brain took another great leap. Blackmail. The only answer. The guy was sticking it to someone. That was the only answer. And, blackmail was one heck of a motive. Someone whacked him to shut him up. But who? And about what?

I turned and stared at my pickup.

What kind of information could a farmhand, a laborer for the distillery, possess that would get him killed? I waited for my brain to take its next great leap, but it tripped over its own feet and fell flat. "Who knows?" I muttered.

I climbed in my truck and sat staring down the road, trying to tiptoe through the labyrinth of confusion in which I had suddenly found myself floundering.

Shaking my head, I started the pickup and headed for Chalk Hills Distillery. First things first. Make sure Morrison and O'Banion knew what I had discovered.

There was no warmth in Beatrice Lenore Morrison's eyes when her butler ushered me into the library, only pained tolerance. Even that turned to ice as I told her what I had dug up. "I know this isn't what you wanted to hear, and I could be wrong, but it appears there is enough questionable evidence to warrant turning the case over to the police. If his death was murder, and we don't turn the information over to the proper authorities, we could both be indicted for obstructing justice."

She arched an eyebrow and sniffed. "And just what is that possibility?" Her tone was heavy with skepticism.

I suppressed a snotty reply at the implication in her tone. After all, she was paying me well, and I hadn't brought her what she wanted. "Probably not much, unless the DA gets his nose out of joint."

A cryptic smile played over her thin lips. "Oh, the District Attorney. Well, suppose you just let me worry about John B. Sowell, Mr. Boudreaux."

"Okay, but I think we need to notify the police."

She looked at me as if my cumulative total of brain cells was about half of normal. "This is only Tuesday. You couldn't have completed your investigation. How can you be absolutely certain it was murder?"

"Everything points that way. At least the way I see it."

"But, are you certain?"

"No. Not beyond reason. But, with some more—"

She interrupted, keeping her cold eyes fixed on mine. "If you are not absolutely positive, then why would you want to discontinue the investigation?"

"I didn't say that. What I'm saying is, I've found information that should be turned over to the police, and let them decide what to do. I don't know if there was a murder or not. But, that appears to be the case. The cops should know about it. Let them take over. You keep me around after that, and you're just wasting money."

"That, Mr. Boudreaux, is not a concern of mine, nor of yours."

"What I mean is that once the police take over, I'm off the case. The cops don't like for guys in my profession to go around sticking our noses in their business. In fact, they go out of their way to remind us to butt out."

She finally pulled her icy glare away from me and stared out the window. The sky was blue, distant hills green, and the graveled parking lot an eye-dazzling white under the afternoon sun. "If you are not one hundred percent certain, Mr. Boudreaux, then I want you to continue. I want you to check and re-check every piece of evidence regardless of how slight."

She turned to face me. "Understand? The police will always be there. Another few days can make no difference to Emmett Patterson. I am paying your company for a thorough report. I'll continue paying your present rate for the length of the investigation, regardless of how long it takes. As I remember, you promised a written report by eight o'clock in the morning."

Reasoning with her was like trying to catch the wind.

"I'll type up a report for you, Mrs. Morrison, but you do understand that I have to tell my boss what I've found?"

"Certainly, certainly. Nevertheless, I wish for you to keep doing whatever it is you sort of people do until you prove his death was simply an accident. It cannot be murder. Just give me weekly reports."

The agency I work for has had a few whacky cases in the past; some we took, some we didn't. But this is America, and even crackpots, if they have the money—especially if they have money—have the right to be afforded fair treatment. Not that she was a crackpot, at least, not certifiable. Still, I wondered if she was holding something back. Did she know something that might help? Otherwise, why throw good money after bad? Made no sense. I'd uncovered enough evidence to warrant police intervention, at least as far as I was concerned. Why was she resisting?

"Mrs. Morrison, is there anything I should know, anything you can tell me about Emmett Patterson that might help, anything that you haven't told me or the police?"

Her eyes narrowed; her jaw stiffened. "Why, what would I know about a common employee?"

I took a deep breath and threw deference aside. "Beats me. Truth is, I figured the reason you're so insistent I continue is you suspect something that you're reluctant to talk about. I got the impression in talking to Mr. Jackson that he wanted to fire Emmett Patterson, but you objected."

Her pales eyes blazed. I stood my ground and added, "Often, Mrs. Morrison, people are hesitant to speak up for fear of involvement. I assure you, anything you tell me stays with me."

For several seconds, she eyed me through cold slits. "And I assure you, Mr. Boudreaux, that I am not used to my integrity being brought to question." She straightened her shoulders and tilted her jaw. "About anything. Especially common laborers with whom I have no association. I leave all those sort of dealings to my supervisors." She spat out the last two words, like exclamation points at the end of a sentence.

We locked eyes. Was she talking about Emmett? Or me? I was growing tired of her high-handed treatment. Except for twelve million dollars, we were the same. Both put our pants, relatively speaking, on one leg at a time.

No, on second thought, I couldn't imagine her putting her pants on one leg at a time. She probably levitated, then lowered herself into her pants. That was how she did it. I shrugged. "If you say so, Mrs. Morrison." I kept my eyes fixed on hers. It had become a contest now to see who broke eye contact first.

She nodded, and I knew she had dismissed me. I considered backing to the door so I could hold her eyes, but while I'm hard-headed and stubborn, I figured I would look foolish backing across the library, dodging chairs and tables, just so I wouldn't take my eyes off her. I dropped my gaze and headed for the door.

Outside, I drove around behind the maintenance barn to Emmett Patterson's cabin, with what I hoped was the combination to his safe burning a hole in my shirt. Maybe I should have refused her offer, but four big ones a day wasn't something to turn down without contacting Marty Blevins, my boss. I knew what Marty would say. He'd utter a few curses then say, "Certainly. Take it. Do whatever she wants. If the rich old broad wants you to mow her yard for four hundred, do it." Old Marty, not a money-hungry bone in his body.

The Yenko Camaro was gone, probably impounded by a wrecker yard that planned on charging outrageous storage rates. Once the charges reached a point exceeding the value of the car, the wrecking yard placed a mechanics lien against it. A painless means of acquiring fine automobiles.

I shut the cabin door and flipped on the light. I hesitated, then locked the door. I didn't want anyone barging in on me. Quickly, I scooted the gun cabinet from the wall.

I gave the dial a spin to clear it, then started dialing. "Let's see. All right, left one, right two, left two . . ." I continued dialing the entire set of sixteen numbers. Despite the sound rationale I had constructed assuring me this was the combination, my doubts grew with each switch in direction.

Finally, I stopped the dial on two, the last digit in the combination. I took a deep breath, flexed my fingers and seized the handle. I whispered a silent prayer and lifted.

The top didn't budge. I yanked harder. Solid as a chunk of granite. Hoping I had made a mistake, I put the combination back in the opposite direction, but with the same results. Deep down, I knew this wasn't the combination, but Louisiana muleheadedness took over and I tried again. Same result.

Muttering a curse, I slammed the heel of my hand against the lock and tried again. Six more times, I dialed the sixteen numbers until finally I sat back on my heels and let out a blast of colorful invectives you'd never hear in polite society.

"It's got to be the combination," I mumbled, staring at the scrap of paper, remembering Claude's remarks about Emmett's penchant for puzzles.

Crossword puzzles were my worst nightmare, so if this was some kind of puzzle, I had as much chance as figuring it out as I had being named Pope Tony the First. I studied the string of numbers. While I'd never delved into the lexical psyche of crossword junkies, I figured they were no different than a sports nut who constantly punctuated his conversation with sporting metaphors. If that was true here, then my string of sixteen numbers was, in all probability, a puzzle.

I sighed.

Chapter Eleven

I headed back to town, driving slowly while I turned the situation over in my head. I laid out my gut feelings, and then tried to punch holes in them. First, Patterson had been black-mailing someone, and chances were, that individual was the one who whacked him.

Second, the killer was at Chalk Hills on Sunday. I had to chuckle at the insight of that conclusion. A no-brainer. That's why Marty had me in missing persons, and Al Grogan as his top sleuth.

Third, the killer had to be one of the employees. There were no guests present at the time of the murder.

My fourth step was to check everyone's bank accounts. That might tell me whom he was milking.

I shrugged and chuckled. Maybe I could enlist the help of Beatrice Morrison's high-powered attorney, William Cleyhorn. Lawyers and bankers seem to play the same golf courses and drink martinis mixed the same way. Naturally, Cleyhorn was out of the question. No way Beatrice would permit him to help me build a murder case, but I had options. Expensive ones, but still, options, such as the good-old-boy network and a few C-notes.

I had forgotten about Katherine Voss, the runaway. She was just a fleeting moment, and I didn't figure she held any cards in the game.

That was another reason I was still in missing persons, and Al Grogan was still the top man. But, I didn't know that at the time.

As I turned down Travis Street to my apartment, I remembered that Jack Edney was still my uninvited guest. I winced. I didn't feel like company tonight. I wanted to be by myself so I could think. Maybe if I called Maggie and told her Jack was sorry, she'd take him back. She fell for the line once a couple of years back. She could have forgotten my previous lies by now.

I opened the door and froze. The setting sun at my back spilled into the dark room, laying a panel of orange across Jack who was lying on the couch, his face half turned to the door. One eye was swollen shut, his lips were split, and his nose was crooked. His shirt and my couch were stained with blood.

At first, I thought he was playing a joke on me. You know, one of those skin-toned masks, but when he slowly rolled his head over and looked at me though his good eye, I knew he wasn't joking. My first thought was that Maggie had whipped up on him good, but I knew better. If Maggie had done it, she would have closed both his eyes. "Jack. What happened?" I flipped on the light and hurried to the couch.

I helped him struggle to sit up. He pressed a bloody rag to his mouth. "Don't know. I answered the door. Two big goons hit me as soon as I opened it. Next thing I knew, I woke up on the floor." He swayed slightly.

"Anything broken?" I laid my hand on his shoulder to steady him.

"Couple of teeth. Top and bottom. They hurt like sin." He gingerly touched the bridge of his nose. "I don't think my nose is busted, but it hurts like it is."

My initial concern for Jack turned to anger. Only one man could be behind such a senseless beating: Danny O'Banion. But his mistake was that his soldiers beat up the wrong guy. They had to be coming after me. I suppressed my anger. "Want something to drink—water, booze?"

"A stiff drink," Jack mumbled through swollen lips. "Real stiff."

I poured us each three fingers of bourbon, wondering what insanity was behind O'Banion's muscle. I handed Jack one and downed the other. "I'll be back," I said, smacking the glass down on the snack bar. "You be all right?"

"You got any pills?"

"In the bathroom. Some painkillers the dentist gave me last year. Hold on." I grabbed a bottle of Tylenol with codeine, and poured him another drink. "Take a couple. That'll help. Hey, take four."

He nodded, almost imperceptibly. "Where you going?"

I didn't have time nor the inclination to explain my destination to Jack. "Back later. And don't call the cops, not yet." I slammed the door behind me. Fire blazed in my eyes. I was ready to kick tail, even Godzilla's if I had to.

I remembered Danny's assurance, *Just look for the black Lexus. That'll be Huey.* Sure enough, the Lexus was parked across the street.

He rolled down the window when he spotted me approaching. "Take me to Danny," I growled. "I'll follow."

Without a change in his bland expression, he pulled away from the curb. I hurried back to my pickup and caught up with him at the light.

Danny's office was on the sixth floor of the Green Light Parking Garage a couple of blocks west of the Convention Center in downtown Austin. One of his goons was stationed at each ramp ascending to the upper floor. Obviously, Danny didn't like walk-in company.

Danny O'Banion looked up at me from behind his desk. He denied the muscle adamantly. "Sure, I've sent mugs out when I had to, but I didn't do this, Tony. That's gospel."

I glanced at Godzilla, I mean Huey, standing next to the door, his barrel-sized arms crossed over his chest. I looked down at Danny. He had no reason to lie. Even if I tried to take him, most I could do was get in one punch before Huey took me apart. Danny knew it, and I knew it. "So, who's behind it? And what's it all about?"

Danny glanced at Huey and gave a terse nod. Silently, the big man left the room. There was a skeptical pitch in his voice. "So, you think there's a possibility that Patterson was murdered, huh?" He gestured to the leather chair behind me. "Sit. Be comfortable."

His question caught me by surprise. I struggled to keep my voice level and deliberate, but my mind was racing. Who had Danny talked to? Morrison? No. Probably Cleyhorn. That's who. Morrison contacted Cleyhorn as soon as I left, and the attorney burned up the phone lines. But, what was his connection with Danny O'Banion? Could Cleyhorn be the contact Danny had mentioned at our first meeting? More questions than I had answers for buzzed around inside my head. "News travels fast," I replied with what I hoped was just the right touch of wry humor.

He grinned crookedly. "Bad news, this time. Why didn't you tell me?"

I leaned back and crossed my legs. "When? I just got in from the old lady's. She doesn't believe me. Wants me to keep digging. I planned on seeing you tonight."

Leaning forward, Danny fixed his eyes on mine. "She's smart. Now, tell me what you found."

"All right, but first, who kicked the blazes out of Jack?"

"Tell me what you found first. I'd like to know why your friend was worked over."

"Fair enough." I told him everything, except about the hidden safe. When I finished, he leaned back, a skeptical expression curling his lips. I knew exactly what he was thinking, so I said it for him. "Yeah. You're right. What I have is mostly speculation, except for the injury on the back of his head. The autopsy report said blunt. The frame of the discs could not have made a blunt injury. The sharp corners would have split the skull."

"Sounds weak to me."

"Not to me."

Danny leaned back and tented his fingers over his chest. "Okay, say it was murder. How did the killer do it?"

"Simple, he rode on the tractor beside Patterson, hit him in the back of the head, and when Patterson fell, the killer jumped off the tractor."

A sly grin curled Danny's lips. "How did he escape the discs?"

"Huh?" I frowned. "What do you mean?"

"The discs were tandem, right? How wide? Thirty feet?"

I hesitated. "How did you know that?"

His grin broadened. "It's my job to know, Tony. Now, stop and think. If the discs are thirty-feet wide . . ."

"Jesus," I muttered, suddenly recognizing his point. If someone had jumped from the tractor, he would have leaped right in front of the discs. "I didn't think of that."

He winked at me. "Think about it. You're the private eye."

His gentle chiding rubbed me the wrong way. "All right, what about his money? The six grand. You tell me, where did he get his money?"

"Drugs. Maybe he was a dealer." Danny shrugged. "Can't tell about anyone these days," he added with a glint of amusement in his eyes. "People got no morals."

I shook my head. "No. The autopsy said the only drug residual in his system was alcohol."

Danny laughed. "Not every dealer is hooked, Tony. You know that."

I grimaced. I'd botched it again, but I wasn't about to admit it. "That's open for debate. Now, who did the job on my friend?"

The smile faded from Danny's lips. "You don't need names, Tony. Trust me on this. What I can tell you is that those who muscled your friend don't want any publicity. They want you to stop. Drop the murder angle. Do the rest of the investigation. Let it go in the books as an accident. You admit yourself that most of what you have is circumstantial. As for the money, well, the guy mighta picked up aluminum cans as a hobby."

"Driving a Yenko Camaro?"

"So, what's a Yenko? Sounds like some kind of lizard."

I chuckled. "An expensive lizard. It's about a thirty-five-thousand-dollar car. Twice that if it's original."

The sarcasm was heavy in his reply. "Maybe he took out a loan." Danny rose and lit a cigarette. He inhaled deeply, then pointed the cigarette at me. The orange glow on the tip faded. "I don't want you hurt, Tony. Listen to me. Forget the murder business."

I started to protest, but he held up his hands, palms out, to stay me. "No one has instructed me to say a thing to you. This is all on my own. I got a call telling me that you had just been reminded that the death was an accident. That was all that was said. That's all that needs to be said. Trust me. Someone passed the word to the big boys and . . ."

"Cleyhorn," I spat out, convinced the attorney was the contact Danny had suggested to his business associates.

Danny shrugged, his expression indifferent. "Who knows? Could be. Anyway, Cleyhorn or someone passed the word to the big boys. They sent you a message. The message was meant for you, not your friend. But you best believe me when I say there will be consequences if we don't listen to them." He drew a deep breath. "And I emphasize *we*."

Sometimes I'm too stubborn for my own good. I suppose I got it from my grandfather who farmed rice in the blacklands of Louisiana. Moise Boudreaux. That was his name. You had to be pigheaded to farm rice. "Gambling with God," he laughed one night as he rocked on the long porch at the old homeplace. He was always in a jovial mood in the evenings after a hard day's work, followed by a solid meal of maque choux, andouille, red beans and rice, all washed down with a couple of glasses of white port.

My temper flared. "Maybe I should take the consequences."

Danny gave me a benevolent grin. His tone became gently supplicating. "Why, Tony? Patterson was nothing to you. You spent two days digging up a lot of circumstantial garbage that the cops wouldn't even spit on. You made eight hundred bucks. The birds are singing, and God's in His heaven. All's right with the world. Step out of this before it blows up on us all."

I grinned at his impromptu eloquence. And he did make some sense. Still I had mixed feelings. I didn't like for anyone to tell me what to do, to make my decisions. That was one of my problems, and I'd paid for my mulishness, more than once. Maybe now was the time to exercise a little discretion, which to my way of thinking was another word for lying. "Tell you what. I'll turn what I got over to my boss. Let him decide."

I watched Danny carefully, trying to see if he believed me or not. I didn't like lying, but I was still a member of the good-guy, bad-guy mindset. I hated to see someone beat the system. On the other hand, I didn't want someone beating on me.

Danny's eyes narrowed, and he started to protest, but I quickly added. "Don't worry. None of what you told me goes beyond this room. I'll just give my boss what I've found, and that's it." I leveled with him. "The truth is, Danny, I figure my boss will want me to stay with her, to prove it was an accident. Four big ones a day pays the rent, and Marty isn't the kind to turn it down. I'll write up a report on everything I found and then let him decide. Whatever he says is fine with me. Okay?" I crossed my fingers. "And if you want, I'll give you a copy and let you and your friends decide on the next step. That oughta make them feel better."

He studied me a moment, his eyes narrow with suspicion. "They ain't jacking around, Tony. Don't press it. Keep on the murder angle, and you won't last two days. If that long."

I winked at him. "I'm no dummy."

He relaxed. "We go back too far, Tony. I don't lie to

you. Be smart. Play the percentages. Just hope your boss does too—for his sake," he added with a leer.

I glanced at my watch. "It's late. I'll see Marty and call you back."

I chewed over the matter during the drive to Marty's apartment. I had mixed emotions. I hated leaving a job half done, but I hated even more the idea of some big goons leaving me half done. I'd long since replaced the philosophical conundrum of bravery versus cowardice with one of practicality. Do what is best at the time. That gem of philosophy was pragmatic, realistic, sensible, and above all else, usually painless.

Still, something about the whole Emmett Patterson scenario disturbed me. I had the feeling that I was looking at the proverbial tip of the iceberg, that beneath the surface lay ninety percent of a story someone didn't want exposed. I tried to push the thought from my head, but I knew it would keep nagging at me until I put it to rest. And the only way I could do that was learn the truth, even if I did nothing with it except satisfy my own curiosity.

By Beatrice Morrison insisting I prove the death an accident, whatever her reason, I had the perfect opportunity. As long as I played it close to the vest.

But, one slip . . . five minutes after Danny's friends figured I was trying to build a murder case, I would be part of the new Interstate.

I was right about Marty. To heck with justice. Where's the money? That was where his interest lay.

"That's all you found?"

"Yeah. But, I think the injury on the head could warrant another look," I added without much conviction.

He shrugged. "Forget it."

Marty Blevins was the epitome of the fictional private eye at home; rumpled, bearded, red-eyed, and toting a glass of bourbon. Now that I think about it, that's usually how he was at work also. That was probably one of the reasons he had been three times divorced and hit with two palimony

suits. Looking at him, I cringed when trying to imagine his
palimony partners. He plopped down on a sagging couch
that groaned under his weight. He glanced expectantly at
my hands. "You write it up yet?"

I remained standing. If you sat with Marty, he expected
you to drink, and while I've nothing against the time-
honored PI tradition of guzzling spirits, I didn't want to get
tied up with him until midnight. I still had to call Danny
with Marty's reply. "I'll type the report tonight. It'll be on
your desk by eight in the morning."

He downed the rest of his bourbon. "Okay. Write it up
and we'll send a copy to the old lady."

"I'll take it out. She asked me to. She told me to keep
snooping around. Like I said, she wants absolute proof the
death was an accident."

He frowned. "She loony or what? The cops already said
it was an accident. Ain't that good enough for her?"

"That's what I told her. I told you before, she wouldn't
listen. Truth is, I can't figure her or her lawyer out either.
But, it's still four hundred a day for the agency."

That got his attention. "Yeah. Hey, what am I griping
about? Go ahead. Take her the report. Saves me postage.
And don't worry about telling the cops what you think."

"You don't think anything is there, huh? I mean, the guy
being murdered." I crossed my fingers waiting for his reply.

"Naw." He shook his head. His jowls flopped.

I felt a sense of relief at his answer. I had turned over
my findings, and my employer didn't want to investigate
the case as murder. Who could complain now? Certainly
not Danny or his bosses. "Okay. See you in the morning."

He struggled to stand.

I waved him down. "I'll show myself out, Marty.
Thanks." I hoped I was doing the right thing.

On the way back to my place, I popped into an HEB
supermarket and grabbed a twelve-pack of Old Milwaukee,
a pizza, then remembered Jack. I grabbed a box of Twin-

kies. Jack probably couldn't chew pizza, but maybe he could gum his way through the Twinkies.

I was right. He was so full of Tylenol and my bourbon that I couldn't understand a word he uttered. His eyes glittered. I glanced at Oscar. The little fish was still alive, still swimming in circles.

"If you're hungry," I said, holding up the box of Twinkies for Jack.

He staggered into the kitchen area after me. He slurred his words. "Whut es y'u go ere?"

I frowned.

He jabbed a finger at the bag. "Whut y'u go ere?"

"Oh, what do I have here?"

Jack nodded.

With a sweep of my arm, I pulled out the pizza. "Pizza. Underways Combination Deluxe Supreme pizza with forty-seven toppings."

He frowned. "How 'bout gumbo?"

I'm no chef, but like many Cajun-born, I can whip up a mean gumbo, and over the years, my gumbos have developed a following in Austin. "No time. Maybe when I finish with this case."

He shook his head, drained his glass, poured another, and staggered back to his couch. I slid the pizza in the microwave, grabbed a beer, and slipped in front of my computer. I booted the machine, and began my report. I'd call Danny later.

Behind me, Jack began snoring. I glanced over my shoulder, on the one hand, irritated at his barging into my house, but on the other, I felt guilty because he had taken the beating meant for me.

Whomever Danny's friends, they meant business. And now, after having a couple of hours to consider the pros and cons of my situation, I was beginning to think maybe I was too curious for my own good; that maybe Marty's decision was the right one despite my own feelings. Take the money and run. Or I did, until I reached the events in my report about Katherine Voss.

Chapter Twelve

Being in my kind of business, the seamy side of a person's life was all I ever saw because everything about crime is dirty and dark, hidden from the light of day. A good investigator always looks for surreptitious motives. They look for the worst in every suspect. They deliberately place every involved individual in the darkest, most suspicious what-if situations. And then they try to find answers.

They regularly put ministers in brothels, teachers in opium dens, drunks in the Governor's office, prostitutes in the church choir. All in an effort to answer some or all of the what-if questions.

When I reached the events concerning Katherine Voss, I asked myself the standard questions. What did happen to the girl? What was she doing at the distillery? Was she home back in Benchmark, Kentucky?

Abruptly, I pulled an Al Grogan, and started thinking. Maybe she was still in the area. Maybe she and Emmett had a thing going. What are the chances she might know something, might be able to shed some light on the mystery? Probably, slim and none, but then, slim and none were the chances for the safe return to Earth for the crew of Apollo 13. And I could have my answer for the minimal cost of a phone call.

Thumbing through my notes, I found the number I'd

copied from the application in Tom Seldes' office. The phone rang eight times before a washed-out, weary voice answered. I asked to speak to Katherine Voss.

I heard a sharp intake of breath, and for several seconds, there was no answer. When the voice replied, it was filled with anger. "Who is this?"

"Tony Boudreaux. Is this Mr. Voss, Mr. Harold Voss?"

The man snapped back. "Yeah, and this ain't my idea of a joke, you lousy, no-good—"

Whoa. I pulled the receiver from my ear and stared at it. What had I stumbled into? I held my temper. "No joke, Mr. Voss. I'm a private investigator in Austin, Texas, and . . ." Quickly I brought him up to date, running my words together so he couldn't interrupt. Naturally, I left out the small scene about her and Patterson making out. But, whatever the sore spot I'd hit with the man, it must have been tender.

"So, I heard Katherine had passed through years back, and I thought she might give me some information about the guy."

Voss hesitated. I knew he was considering my explanation, so I added in a conciliatory tone. "I'm not trying to cause any trouble, Mr. Voss. I'm just looking to do my job. May I speak with her, please?"

I hardly recognized the voice that replied. Instead of the anger-packed shouts that had been spewed at me, I was suddenly listening to a weak, broken man. "I'm sorry, Mr. Boudreaux. It's just that . . ." His voice quivered. "She . . . Katherine, that is, never . . . she never came back. We never found her. My . . . my wife died heartbroken eight years ago. The child was the light of her life . . . of both our lives. She left for Texas and then just dropped out of sight."

He paused.

Even though I had no way of knowing the situation, I cursed myself for the pain I had resurrected in the man. I didn't know what to say. I couldn't patronize Voss by telling him I knew how he felt. Christ, he'd probably heard those trite words every day for the past ten years. I just whispered, "Yes, sir."

His voice dropped into a monotone. "She never came back, Mr. Boudreaux. I figure she's probably dead somewhere. If she was alive, she would have called. She wasn't a wild child. In fact, she was pretty level-headed. She just wanted to see more than these Kentucky hills and our one-horse business."

I could hear the emotion building in his voice as he continued about his missing daughter. "You know, she wanted to live a little before coming back here and settling down, and taking over the business. That's what me and her had talked about for years. She just wanted to live a little first. That's the way kids are today."

"Yeah. I know." I asked a perfunctory question of the grieving man. "What kind of business do you have, Mr. Voss?"

"Just a small distillery. Small batch of sour mash whiskey. Nothing like the big boys, but we do enough local business to live comfortably." He chuckled. "Katherine always swore she wanted us to become a national brand, and then world wide." His voice cracked, and a sob caught in his throat. "She had the determination to do it too, Mr. Boudreaux. And I ain't saying that just because she's my daughter. But she had a spark that I never had. She coulda done it. She coulda made this hayseed plant into a respected distillery." His voice cracked again. "Oh, Jesus," he sobbed. "Oh, Jesus. My little girl. My little girl."

"Mr. Voss. I'm very sorry I called and stirred up all that hurt. If I'd known, why . . ."

There came a short silence. Then, "No way for you to know, son. I . . . I wish I could help you with your problem, but I can't."

"Thank you, sir. Good night."

"Mr. Boudreaux. Just one more second. If . . . if you do find out anything, anything at all about my Katherine, I'd appreciate you lettin' me know. You got no idea how many nights I've laid awake thinking about her laying out in some forest or field just crumbling to dust until nothing is left. That ain't no way for a soul to spend eternity. If she is dead, I'd like to bury her by her mother."

I grimaced. "Don't worry, Mr. Voss. If I learn anything, you'll be the first to hear."

"Thank you. Thank you. I'm just an old man now with nothing left but to find out the truth about my little girl. Please, please, do what you can."

I went back to my report. Katherine Voss. A dead end. No connection with Patterson. I shook my head, remembering Hawkins' story about Emmett and Voss making out behind the rackhouse. "Well, no connection as far as his murder," I muttered.

Suddenly, I was struck by the coincidence of the young woman leaving one distillery and showing up at another. Happenstance? Fortuity? Serendipity? Or by design? My pulse picked up. I felt that old curiosity welling up inside.

Thumbing quickly through my notes on Katherine Voss, I noted that she had filled out the application on June 18, 1988. The odds were a thousand to one, but could she have come to Chalk Hills Distillery for a purpose? Maybe she wanted to study the operation, then take the knowledge back to Kentucky. More than one entrepreneur had pirated competition.

But, what was worth stealing around here?

The question rang a bell. I thumbed back through my notes. "Jesus. I wonder if this is it?" I read aloud the notes from my interview with Alonzo Jackson. "One of a kind, it is a pure culture yeast, Saccharomyces Cerevisiae, developed from a single original cell and carefully propagated and maintained until a vigorous strain was produced with its own particular properties to produce whiskey possessing desired characteristics. We made our first breakthrough in nineteen-eighty-eight, and since that time, we have constantly striven to improve the yeast."

I stared at the notebook. My brain raced. I muttered, trying to verbalize my thoughts. "What if she came to

Chalk Hills to steal the formula, or some of the culture? That could explain why she was here." I knew I was stretching the envelope, but stranger things have happened.

If only I knew when she left home. I looked at the telephone, reluctant to disturb Voss again. She might not have known about the yeast. She could have simply wanted to see the world, and someone who wants to ramble takes his time. She could have hit New Orleans and remained for months before moving on. But, what if there was only a couple of weeks between the time she left Kentucky and the day she arrived at Chalk Hills? That would indicate some degree of deliberation.

I studied the telephone, then grabbed it and quickly dialed the number. If I didn't find out when she left, I'd never stop worrying over it.

Voss answered, his voice weak and old.

"Sorry to bother you again, Mr. Voss. This is Boudreaux. Can you tell me when Katherine left home. The date, more or less?"

Woodenly, he replied, "I'll never forget that day. I drove her down to the Greyhound station in Benchmark. That morning. June fifteen, nineteen-eighty-eight."

I held my voice steady as I thanked him, but my hands were shaking when I replaced the receiver. June 15. Three days before she showed up at Chalk Hills. Three days. On the Greyhound bus. How many ways can you spell deliberate?

More and more loose threads were showing up in the case. It was like a pebble in a pond. The ripples spread until they covered the entire surface.

I had the feeling Chalk Hills was the pebble. Katherine Voss was one ripple. Patterson was another. Patterson was dead. What about Voss? She had vanished ten years earlier. Where? A grim thought hit me. The notion was outrageous, absurd, but I couldn't shake it. Finally, I gave in to the idea. After all, it was just conjecture, another game of what if.

Suppose there were two murders? And if so, did one

have anything to do with the other? Abruptly, two pieces of puzzle slipped together. What if something had happened to Voss while she was at Chalk Hills? Patterson might have known about it, and decided to use that knowledge for a little blackmail.

I nodded slowly. Men have been killed for a lot less.

Behind me, Jack snorted and gurgled.

My heart thudded. I dragged my tongue over my dry lips. "What I need is a drink," I muttered, rising and heading for the kitchen. "A stiff one."

I leaned back against the snack bar, sipping my drink and gathering my thoughts. First, I had no hard proof of any crime; none that Voss was even dead; none that Patterson had been murdered. And sound theories need facts for support.

One thing was certain, I told myself, staring hard at the half-empty glass in my hand. I wanted the truth, for me, and for Harold Voss, and for Emmett Patterson and yes, for Katherine Voss. At the same time, I didn't care to end up in the cornerstone of a skyscraper somewhere, or under the playing field at Giant Stadium rubbing shoulders with Jimmy Hoffa.

I shook the glass, swirling the golden liquid. I wondered if I was good enough to pull it off. Could I find out the truth without getting myself killed?

I grunted and lifted the glass to my lips. Hesitating, I stared at the amber liquid. The last thing I needed was a brain addled by alcohol. I sat the glass down. "First things first," I muttered, going back to my computer. I'd write up the report, a very innocuous report, for Marty. He'd file it away, and I'd go back out to Chalk Hills to see if I could find some answers for the questions that were beginning to nag at me. I could use the pretense of the investigation for a few more days.

One thing for sure, I reminded myself, I had to be careful about the information I provided Beatrice Morrison, for she would pass it along to Cleyhorn, who in turn would give it to Danny O'Banion's bosses. If they thought I was even considering a murder case, they would move fast. And there was no chance I could get out of their way in time. The only information they would get from me was growing evidence that the death was accidental.

For a moment, I wondered about the size of the investment Danny's friends had in the distillery, but I realized the amount of money made no difference. Danny's bosses were the kind who did not like to lose money, even pocket change.

And I couldn't forget Danny. I knew he had Huey, alias Godzilla, tailing me, which meant that everything I did, I had to have a logical explanation that would satisfy him.

I continued working on the benign report for Marty, making certain I had enough unanswered questions to justify continuing the investigation. At the same time, I made no allusions to murder.

When I finished the report, in which I recommended an additional week of investigation just to make sure of the facts, I called Danny and read it to him. I didn't like lying, and I had no idea just what I would do if my suspicions proved true. But, one thing was certain, I had to follow through on my hunch.

Then I would worry about what came afterward.

I felt like a knight beginning his quest for the Holy Grail, except most of those poor chumps got themselves chopped up with a broadsword or fried to a crisp by the local dragon.

Jack stumbled into the kitchen the next morning as I was pouring water in the coffeepot. He clutched his jaw with one hand, and his swollen eye had taken on a deep purple glaze. "How you feel?"

He grimaced. "Don't ask. I gotta get to the dentist this morning." He popped a couple more Tylenol with codeine in his mouth. "Find out who did this?"

"Yeah." I looked around at him. "Hey, man. I'm sorry. They were after me. I feel guilty. I'll pay for the dentist."

He tried to grin. "Forget that. I got insurance. It was my fault for being here." He climbed up on a bar stool and eyed the coffee hungrily. "Soon as I finish at the dentist, I'll go down and report it to the cops."

I winced. "Not a good idea, Jack. There's a lot of heat out there. Like I said, you were an accident." I hesitated. "I don't know the whole story yet. Do me a favor. Hold off on the cops until I find out just what is taking place."

He looked at me with his one good eye. "You serious?"

"As a busted leg."

He considered my request soberly. Gingerly, he touched a finger to his lip, then glanced at his leg. With a resigned shrug, he replied. "If you say so."

After leaving a copy of the report with Marty, I picked up some film for my camera, a Fuji 35, and headed out to Chalk Hills. I mentally tabulated a list of specific objectives I wanted to accomplish that morning. First, drop off the report to Mrs. Morrison. Second, pictures of the interior of Patterson's cabin. If the numbers I had found in his wallet were a cryptographic puzzle, maybe something in his cabin would provide a key. Third, more details about Katherine Voss, starting with Seldes, then the Master Distiller, Emeritus, Alonzo Jackson, and finally talk Carrie Jean into getting me in to quiz someone at the Medical Examiner's office about the injury to the back of Patterson's skull.

Like a pit bull, I hung tenaciously to my theory, refusing to believe the injury was incurred by a fall instead of a club.

I topped the rise above Chalk Hills. The distillery appeared deserted, but I knew better. I gunned the Chevy pickup and sped down the hill.

As I passed the maintenance barn, David Runnels stood in the doorway, wiping his hands with a rag and staring at me. I gave him a cursory, two-finger wave and angled toward the main house.

Beatrice Morrison read the report, thanked me, and promptly dismissed me with the reminder to report again in one week. Like the hired help I was, I nodded. "One week."

Patterson's cabin was just as I had left it. I'd already given it a thorough look, so I didn't plan on wasting time searching again. Throwing open the door and raising the blinds, I proceeded to shoot thirty-six exposures of the interior, trying to place the shots so that I could piece the final prints into a panoramic sweep of the room.

Next, I visited David Runnels, who seemed puzzled that I was still around. "Figured to have seen the last of you."

"Couple of odds and ends for Mrs. Morrison. Nothing major. I probably will have it all wrapped up in a couple more days."

He snorted, his bulldog face twisted in a sneer. "Emmett wasn't worth another couple of days."

"Maybe not, but Mrs. Morrison is paying me to finish up, and that's what I'm planning on doing." I looked around the barn. "You sure keep this equipment looking good, almost like it was straight off the showroom floor."

He turned to his machines and beamed. "Well, like I told you before, that's my job."

I studied him. He was a strong man, strong enough to have wielded the club that knocked Patterson from the tractor. But then I remembered the tandem discs. They sat in one corner of the barn, two thirty-foot rows of shiny disc blades with edges like a knife.

Some quick mental calculations pointed out that if someone leaped from the tractor, he had only a couple of seconds to cover fifteen or so feet before the discs rolled over him. Tough job. The slightest stumble or hesitation meant death.

Runnels interrupted my thoughts. "Anything else?"

"Huh, oh, yeah. That girl that came through here about ten years back. Remember her?"

He looked around at me. "What about her?"

"Nothing. Just curious. Thought I might try to look her up and see if she knows anything."

He shook his head in amusement. "How could she? That was ten years ago."

I pulled out my notebook and thumbed through it. "Yeah, but you told me she and Emmett had a thing going. I—"

"No. I didn't say nothing about them having anything to do with each other. I don't know if they did. All I said was he flirted with her."

So much for my attempt to finesse information from him about Katherine Voss. "Oh, yeah. Sorry." I glanced at my notebook. "It was Claude who said they had something going. But, you did threaten him over her, right? A fight or something?"

His bulldog face darkened. He held his temper, but his voice quivered when he replied. "So, I blew up. I never touched him. Besides, I still don't see why you're so interested in that girl?"

I looked at him from under my eyebrows. "I just figure that maybe she moved into town, and he kept seeing her." I was still fishing for any kind of lead, but I didn't get a bite.

Runnels grunted. "May have. I got no idea, and I don't care."

With a nod, I stepped back. "Well, I've bothered you enough. I'll let you get back to work."

Tom Seldes was rolling an oaken barrel onto a forklift when I entered the rackhouse. He eyed me suspiciously, then positioned the barrel on the forks.

I didn't ask Seldes any questions, not directly. Instead, I told him of my conversation with Voss, hoping to elicit additional information from him, a sly ploy that failed miserably.

"Mr. Voss sent his thanks to you and the others here for looking after his daughter while she was here." It was a lie, but I didn't want him to think I was still snooping.

Seldes grunted and positioned the barrel again. "I didn't do nothing." He nodded to the forklift driver, who backed away and disappeared into the shadows of the rackhouse with the barrel.

"Well, you sent her to Jackson when you couldn't use

her," I replied, noting how easily he had manhandled the barrel. He was another who could have swung the club, but why? What reason could the muscular man have? "You could have just run her off the place."

He considered my remark. "Yeah, suppose you're right, but like I told you before, she wanted to see Lonny. Besides, that was ten years ago."

"One more question. You know Mary Tucker?"

"Sure. Why?"

"Was she here Sunday?"

He thought a moment. "I didn't see her, but her car was here."

"Oh?"

"Yeah."

I waited for him to continue, but he just stared at me. I pulled out my faithful notebook. "Just another couple of minutes of your time, if you don't mind. I'd like to go back over our previous conversation for my report to Mrs. Morrison."

The broad-shouldered man shrugged and reached for another barrel beside the wall. He tilted it and rolled it easily to the middle of the floor. "You talking about that report you just gave her?"

His unexpected question knocked the breath from me. I scrambled to cover my blunder. "Yeah. I just want to be sure everything I told her was right. I should have doublechecked before, but she was anxious for the report."

It was a lame explanation. He gave me a smug grin, and I knew he didn't believe me. "Oh," was all he said. I asked a few perfunctory questions just to save face, which he answered with the same arrogant grin on his face.

After I left Seldes, I visited Mary Tucker in the maintenance barn, and went nowhere. She vaguely remembered me from the Red Grasshopper on Monday, and she knew nothing about the girl. But she did reiterate, in colorful obscenities, her unbounded delight that Patterson was dead, and suggest a couple of crude means for the disposition of his body. And yes, she replied defiantly, she was away from the distillery on Sunday despite what Tom Seldes said. "Every car out here is red. He mighta seen the forklift and thought it was mine."

From the barn, I headed to the Master Distiller's office, toying with the fact that Seldes claimed to have seen Tucker's car even though she insisted she was nowhere around. Who was lying? Or was it an honest mistake?

I had also learned one more puzzling fact. For whatever reason, Beatrice Morrison had made it known to Tom Seldes that I had delivered the report. Why him? And why so fast? I would have thought the report would have gone to William Cleyhorn first, not the foreman of the rackhouses. From Runnels, I had learned nothing new.

I was going in circles, like Oscar, my brain-damaged Tiger Barb.

Chapter Thirteen

I hesitated at the bottom of the stairs. Sometimes I have trouble piecing together my own logic in any kind of coherent sequence; consequently, I often find myself envying those who can. I've come to the conclusion that logical thinking is in the genes, and that only ten percent of the deductive process can be taught. Those like me, who are ninety percent impulse, can only stumble and blunder ahead.

To be honest, I've read all of Sherlock Holmes, and I can't believe anyone could possibly be so perceptive and intuitive except in fiction. From a spot of mud on a woman's cuff, the renowned detective's perceptive deduction that she had been riding in the right-hand seat of a dog cart traveling along Cambridge Road at two-thirty Sunday, stretches credibility more than trying to stretch your bottom lip over your head.

On the other hand, I do, from time to time, amaze myself with unexpected flashes of logic, just as I did when I looked up the stairs to the Master Distiller Emeritus' door and realized that I was getting nowhere.

All the questions had been asked, and all the answers had been given. I had learned nothing fundamentally new from Runnels or Seldes or Tucker. With the exception of Tucker's vehicle possibly being on the distillery grounds on Sunday, both men provided me with the same facts as they had earlier. I wasn't asking the right questions because I'd run out of information on which to base my questions, and until I did some more digging, I wouldn't know what to ask.

So, what did I need to learn?

First, I wanted to find out if my theory that Emmett Patterson could have been murdered held water. Maybe I had misinterpreted the head injury? Second, had Katherine Voss come to Chalk Hills deliberately? And if she did, why? What could have been so tempting to make her travel over seven hundred miles? I had an idea, but I needed proof.

If I got the right answer on both questions, then I would know I wasn't chasing rabbits.

I'm sure ace investigator Al Grogan would not have been running in circles like me, but that's why he's where he is, and I'm in missing persons.

I spun on my heel and headed back to the pickup.

Just as I reached the door, Alonzo Jackson's soft, reticent voice stopped me. "Did you wish to see me, Mr. Boudreaux?"

I looked up the stairs. He was staring down at me, a slight smile on his lips. He still wore the Band Aid. That must have been some cut. I shook my head. "Not today, Mr. Jackson. I'll get back with you if I need to."

He nodded slowly. "Anyway I can help."

"Thanks."

Pulling into a Qwik-Stop Photo Shop next to Safeway on Lamar Boulevard in north Austin, I dropped off the roll of film I'd taken in Patterson's cabin, and opted for the two-hour service. While the film was being developed, I planned to visit the Travis County Forensics Lab again, and see if Carrie Jean could wrangle me a few minutes with one of the technicians in the Medical Examiner's office.

Traffic was more congested than a summer head cold. To make matters worse, pedestrians ignored the traffic, darting through the lines of creeping automobiles. I tried the air conditioning on the outside chance it might seize the moment and function. It didn't, so I did the next best thing and cursed.

Sometimes luck strolls in and decides to take a hand. Other times, it strolls right on past the door, leaving you to fight the battle yourself. My grandfather always told me, "Boy, one thing for sure about luck, it'll change when you least want it to, but it will change." I had to grow up some to understand what he meant, but when I did, I firmly embraced the idea. I never counted on luck. That way I wasn't disappointed.

But, luck took my side at the lab.

"You hit paydirt today. Carl and Spitz are on duty. They're the techs who assist the ME, but if you want the truth, they know more about the job than he does," Carrie Jean whispered, glancing around her brightly lit, but empty office. "The girls are in the lounge for lunch. The techs eat in the examining room."

"With the stiffs?"

She shrugged and gave me a wry grin. "At least it's quiet."

Sure enough, at a corner table in the chilly room, two technicians were taking a brown-bag lunch break. One poured iced tea from a thermos. Across the room, a cadaver lay on a stainless steel gurney, a cloth draped modestly over his genitals. The bluish cast beneath his pale skin reminded me of a frozen chicken.

The mixed odor of pine oil and formaldehyde hung heavy in the lab. At one end of the room was a series of stainless steel sinks and on one of the sink aprons, rows of plastic bags containing samples for the pathology lab.

Carrie Jean introduced us.

Carl was short, fat, bald, and bearded. Spitz was of average build, wore a mushroom haircut, and his face had been scarred by the mother-of-all-acne outbreaks.

"Sit," said Carl, offering me a carrot stick. "Have some lunch."

I glanced at the cadaver, whose bony legs were about the same diameter as Carl's carrot stick. "No, thanks. I just ate." My stomach growled as I sat, and both men laughed.

"Hey." Spitz laughed. "My first few days here, I must've lost twenty pounds. No appetite. But, you get used to it." He spooned some chicken noodle soup between his thin lips. A stray noodle slapped against his chin. He sucked it into his mouth with a loud slurp and chuckled. "Carl hates for me to do that."

Carl shook his head wearily.

Carrie Jean patted my shoulder. "I'll see you later. I've got to get back to my desk." She winked at the techs. "He's an old flame, boys. Treat him nice."

They all laughed.

"So, old flame," said Carl, biting another chunk of carrot after Carrie closed the door behind her. "What can we do for you?"

Quickly, I explained.

Spitz grimaced. "Oh, yeah. Patterson. You remember, Carl. He was that pile of corned beef hash we had in here."

The grin faded from Carl's pudgy face. "Christ. What a way to go."

The odor in the lab was getting to me. I swallowed hard and decided to skip the idle chitchat. "Look, fellas. I've really just got one question. The injury to his head. I think you said it was a blunt trauma."

Carl looked at me curiously. "How do you know what we said? You see the report?"

I studied them a moment, reading the friendly amusement in their eyes. "Let's say I dreamed it or heard it somewhere. All I need to know is what you think caused it?"

They looked at each other, and Spitz shook his head. "I can't remember. Is that what we put on the report?"

Carl growled. "How can you forget that guy?" He touched the back of his head. "There was a blunt trauma right about here. When he fell off the tractor, his head struck something hard. From what we've learned since he came in, the guy must've hit the frame of the tandem disc. That's it. No big secret."

I considered my next question. "If you'd seen that kind of trauma elsewhere, what would you say caused it?"

Both techs frowned.

I explained. "Say, someone came in from off the street, and he had that sort of injury. What would you say did the damage?"

Carl shrugged. "Well, it could be anything round and smooth. I'd say a ball bat would do it, wouldn't you, Spitz?"

"Suppose so. Maybe something just a little larger than the bat. Why? You know something?"

"Not me." I laughed, but I was remembering the interior of Claude Hawkins' cabin. Pure baseball. A picture of the bleached bat on the wall flashed into my head. "The cops know more than I do." A glib lie leaped to my lips. "The truth is, and don't laugh, I've been working on a novel. My first. And I'm trying to find out ways to mislead my readers." It was an imaginative fabrication, and to my surprise, it worked.

"A writer, huh?"

"Wannabe. This accident at the distillery got me to thinking," I replied, rising and offering my hand. "Hey, guys. Thanks. You've told me what I needed."

Spitz nodded. "Anytime. You gonna put us in the dedication of the book?"

"Sure. You bet." I hesitated, remembering Mary Tucker and the others out at the distillery. "Okay, say, for sake of my novel, someone was murdered like that. Is it possible from looking at the injury to tell if it was done by a man or woman?"

Spitz and Carl looked at each other. "Yeah," Carl said. "Well, not exactly, but you can made an educated guess. Take Patterson. If I saw that kind of injury, I'd guess a woman did it or a puny man. To be honest, I don't think the blow was hard enough to knock the guy out." He grimaced, and his tone became sober. "And I don't think the fall knocked him out. I think the poor slob was conscious when he fell under those blades."

"Christ," Spitz put in.

I cringed at Carl's observation. "Gives me the creeps."

Spitz arched an eyebrow. "Think what it did to him."

"Yeah." I shook my head. "In other words, if you had to say the injury was caused by a person, chances are it would be a woman?"

"I'd say so." Carl pursed his lips. "I saw a case once where a man hit another. Crushed the skull. The impact bruised the brain. We didn't see much of that on Patterson."

Spitz grunted. "At least, from what we could tell by what we had. He was a mess."

"Thanks, guys. Now, one more question. Suppose I used a piece of lumber to whack someone on the head, say a two-by-two, you know with the square corners. What kind of impression would that leave?"

"Different." Carl made a concave sweep with his hand. "A baseball bat makes one like this, but if you used a club with square corners, then it would leave an impression like this. He brought the edge of his hand straight down, then cut it at a ninety-degree angle. "That's what they call a penetrating trauma. Your other one is like you said, a blunt trauma."

I nodded. The pieces were slowly falling in place. "Thanks again, fellas." I grinned to myself. A baseball bat. And I knew just where to look.

I closed the door behind me and glanced around the office. Across the room, Carrie Jean was leaning over one of the computer operator's shoulders studying the monitor. She looked up, and I blew her a kiss. She winked, and I hurried outside, anxious to get back to my apartment and start building my case.

Danny O'Banion and his bosses popped into my head. No surprise there. There's no way I could forget men who repay their debts by burying some poor chump in a foundation.

I knew I was working against time. Sooner or later, someone would start wondering why I was spending so much time on the case. All I could do was remind them that Beatrice Morrison was paying me to prove Emmett Patterson's death was an accident. But, I had to move fast. You can tread water for just so long.

I picked up the developed film, a sack of eight burgers and fries, and headed back to the apartment, anxious for the comfort of air conditioning, but dreading the presence of Jack Edney. I chided myself for being so selfish. After all, he'd probably be out of my hair by now if he hadn't taken the beating that was meant for me. If I weren't such a self-centered jerk, I would be considerate and gracious for the involuntary sacrifice on his part.

Jack reclined on the couch, his feet propped on the coffee table. Thanks to a heavy dose of lidocaine administered at the dentist, one side of his face drooped, forcing him to drink through a straw.

"You still alive, huh?"

He nodded slowly, gently touching his fingers to his jaw.

I held up the sack. "Burgers. Can you eat?"

"You bet," he mumbled, trying to force his numbed lips to function. "One way or another. I'm starving."

While I opened a beer, he told me about the visit to the dentist. Two root canals and temporary caps.

"Talked to Maggie?" I unwrapped a burger and splashed catsup on the fries, hoping the warring couple had made up. I liked my privacy, and even a good friend like Jack Edney became worrisome after a time. Ben Franklin said it best: "Fish and visitors smell after three days."

His cheek bulging like a chipmunk's, Jack shook his head. "I'm going to give her a call this evening. I don't want to impose on you any longer, old buddy."

A flood of guilt engulfed me. "Glad to," I replied, willing at the moment to let him stay for a month to assuage the guilt and self-reproach I felt. "Sorry about the beating."

Jack was one of those rare souls with an irrepressible sense of humor and a thick skin. "It coulda been worse. Maggie could have done it." His words were slurred, but animated. His good eye twinkled.

I laughed. "What are you, some kind of comedian?"

"Yeah. That's what caused our problem. I wanted to enter a stand-up comic contest at Borgia's down on Sixth Street, but Maggie didn't want me to. You know how it goes. One word leads to another, and suddenly, there's a full-scale war going on."

"A stand-up comic?" I studied him a moment. I'd never pictured Jack in that role, but now that I considered it, with his bounce and good humor and his complete disregard of pointed insults, he might be darned good. "What made you think about that?"

"I listen to them all the time. I'm better than some already. Some of those bums stumble all over the punchline for their joke. And they get paid."

"And Maggie didn't like the idea, huh?" I washed a chunk of hamburger down with a swallow of cold beer.

"Naw. She thought I'd embarrass us or that word might get back to the school, and I'd get fired or something."

I chuckled. Sometimes, it was hard to understand a woman's logic. How could it embarrass her if she wasn't on the stage with Jack? And no way a school could get rid of a teacher today for working a bar. In fact, only theft or morals would get one dismissed. Even incompetence in the classroom was insufficient for termination.

"What are you laughing about?"

"Nothing. Just women. Can't live with them . . ."

Grinning, Jack added, "And you sure can't drown them, which reminds me of some of history's most famous presidential statements."

I rolled my eyes. "Forget it. I got work to do."

Chapter Fourteen

J ack kept up a constant stream of chatter, but after his first set of jokes, I shut him out, concentrating on the information I'd picked up at the lab. If someone had indeed struck Patterson with a ball bat or club, the ME techs believed the perp was more likely to be a woman. But, that didn't make sense. The only woman at the distillery was Mary Tucker, who swore she was not present Sunday, even though Seldes claimed he saw her car.

There was another woman at the distillery, I reminded myself. Beatrice Morrison. Of course, there was Janice, my sometimes Significant Other, but she was with me.

However, I could not visualize the matronly Morrison climbing up on a tractor, whopping Patterson on the back of his head, then leaping from the tractor. As old and fragile as she appeared, she'd break into a dozen pieces before the discs reached her.

That left Mary Tucker. And she had the perfect motive. Emmett Patterson had seduced her daughter, caused the girl to abort, and then by his very presence, driven the girl from her mother. But, according to my notes, David Runnels said she had not been on the distillery premises on the Sunday Patterson died, did not come in Sunday night, and never punched in on Monday. On the other hand, Seldes claimed

118

he saw her car, the red Honda, on Sunday. But Tucker herself swore she was gone.

Who was lying?

Jack broke into my thoughts. "So, what do you think, huh?"

I blinked. "About what?"

His forehead wrinkled in a disappointed frown. "About my routine. My monologue."

"Oh. Yeah, good, good," I muttered, turning back to my notes.

"You weren't paying attention."

I sighed. "Yeah, I was, Jack. It's just that I got a lot on my mind. Okay?" I glanced at the packet of film.

Then he started pouting.

I almost laughed. The subtlety of pouting wasn't too effective with lips still numb from lidocaine, and an eye swollen shut.

"It isn't funny," he muttered, sliding off the bar stool and stomping back to the couch, but not before he grabbed another beer from the refrigerator and three hamburgers from the bag.

Ignoring his hurt feelings, I spread the film on the snack bar and arranged it as if I was standing in the door looking into the cabin. I had no idea what I was looking for. Perhaps, I figured, whatever it was would jump out at me and shout, "Here I am."

It didn't.

I went over each picture carefully, studying each item. Thirty minutes later, I leaned back in frustration, sick of staring at horns, belts, western shirts, lamps, clocks, couches, and gun cabinets. I pulled out my notebook and studied the numbers again: 1210841084284212. One thing for sure, that wasn't the combination.

Across the editorial page of the morning *Daily Press*, I jotted the numbers down in pairs, 12, 10, 84, 10, 28, 42. Nothing. Next, I pulled out other combinations and came up with two 12s, two 10s, three 8s, one 28, one 41, two

42s, and three 84s. I shook my head. They had nothing in common.

I put them in threes, fours, and fives. Still no relationship. I wrote them backwards, sideways, and upside down. Nothing.

I muttered a curse, crumpling the newspaper in my hand and throwing it in the trash. "You're going nowhere, and fast, Tony."

I yanked a bottle of Jim Beam Black Label from the cabinet, gulped a couple of swallows, popped the cap on an Old Milwaukee, and washed the bourbon down. I stared out of the kitchen window several moments, gathering my thoughts, feeling the warmth of the sudden surge of alcohol hit my bloodstream.

I've always been a great believer in brainstorming. Jot down any idea, regardless of how bizarre. Sometimes it worked. Sometimes it didn't. So, with my faithful pencil in hand, I grabbed another page of the *Daily Press* and began making a list of what I had, or at least, what I thought I had.

I jotted my ideas down in outline form, you remember, the format old lady Watson insisted on in tenth-grade English. For every 1, there's a 2. For every A, there's a B.

One. Motive for killing Emmett Patterson. There could be four. A. Blackmail. How did he sock away six thousand, plus drive a Yenko? B. Seduction. The possibility that Harold Voss had somehow been involved in retaliation for the seduction of his daughter. C. Vengeance. Mary Tucker getting her dues on the man who impregnated her daughter, then aborted her grandchild and drove her daughter away. D. Anger. Claude Hawkins lost his Silverado pickup because of Patterson.

Two. Why did Katherine Voss come to Chalk Hills?
A.
No A. None that I could think of.

I considered the blackmail motive. Since Cleyhorn appeared to be hand-in-glove with Danny O'Banion's bosses, I couldn't get his help to check bank accounts. That meant

I had to fall back on Old Faithful and come up with some cash.

I reached for the phone and punched in a number. My man, Eddie Dyson, Old Faithful, was visiting Houston. "Dunno." The dull voice on the other end of the line slurred his words. "Probably next couple of days. You wanta leave'm a message?"

"Yeah." I left a message.

Eddie had never disappointed me. I don't know how he found his information. The truth is, I didn't want to know. With Eddie, the old aphorism, *the less you know, the better off you are*, is a veritable fact. And if it isn't an aphorism, it should be with Eddie. I jotted myself a note on one of those small stick-um pads and posted it on the computer monitor. I would try Eddie the next morning.

Next on the list was seduction. Harold Voss retaliating against Patterson. That wouldn't hold water. Voss hadn't heard from his daughter, so how could he have known what took place at Chalk Hills?

I made a large, dark X through seduction.

Vengeance next, and that could be Mary Tucker, who swore she wasn't at the distillery on Sunday. If the truth was known, the woman was probably so stoned, she had no idea where she might have been.

Despite the problem Danny posed for the killer having to leap from the moving tractor, she was still a suspect if she didn't have an alibi. That was one of my next steps, to check her alibi.

Then there was the anger motive. Claude Hawkins lost his Silverado pickup because of Patterson. In Texas, a pickup is almost as close to a man as his wife. And, Claude had access to a baseball bat. But, could anyone be dumb enough to use one of his own ball bats in a murder? My answer, after having visited with Claude, was a resounding yes. And he was probably dumb enough to leave the blood on it as a fashion statement, though I didn't spot anything that looked like blood when I interviewed him.

But, there was a bleached bat on the wall. I stared into space, wondering how to get my hands on it.

On the other hand, when Patterson started crying, Claude wimped out, he said. And that was after his Silverado had been repossessed. I had a gut feeling he wasn't the one. Where would he get the kind of blackmail money Patterson was obviously receiving? Still, I wanted to get my hands on that bat.

The second reason I discounted Claude as the perp was the ME technicians' opinion the blunt trauma was more likely caused by a woman than a man. So, I made another X, a light one across Claude Hawkins.

That left Tucker or whomever Patterson had been blackmailing.

I looked at the subject of number 2 on my outline. Katherine Voss, an unknown. True, it appeared she came straight from Benchmark, Kentucky to the Chalk Hills Distillery by Greyhound bus. Such an undeviating journey indicated some purpose. What purpose? Maybe if I knew that, then I'd know the next question to ask.

I leaned back and stared at my notes. The way my luck ran, I would spend hours and days searching for her, only to discover she had settled in San Antonio, and for whatever reason, decided not to let anyone know where she was.

Still, I wanted to know more about her, about her reasons for showing up at Chalk Hills. No one at the distillery could help, or would help. Then I remembered the idea that had jumped into my head after talking to Harold Voss. What if she had come to Chalk Hills to steal the formula, or some of the culture the distillery had developed? But how could she have known about it?

"Obviously, stupid," I growled to myself. "She read it or saw it on TV."

TV archives could be accessed, but not without some difficulty, plus a hundred bucks an hour for research, and another hundred for a video. So, for the time being, that left newspapers and the library.

A shaft of sunlight lanced across the newspaper. I

glanced at the blinds. It was late. I checked the time and grimaced. Rush-hour traffic. Almost impossible to go anywhere in Austin at this time of day without getting caught up in traffic jams, dodging mushroom heads sky high on speed, or fighting off homeless beggars at every corner with signs reading WORK FOR FOOD.

I wanted to visit the Perry-Castaneda Library on the University of Texas campus. Check the newspapers back in the spring of 1988. I reasoned that if something brought Katherine Voss to Austin, the newspaper and magazine were the logical delivery systems.

Then I had another flash of inspiration. The Internet. I had a local server for which service I paid $19.95 a month, unlimited access. I'd been online for a couple of years, but still felt like an Arkansas backwoodsman from a hick county where everyone had the same DNA.

I went into the living room and, despite the scorching glare from Jack, booted up the machine and went online. I reasoned it would be simple to find the *Austin Daily Press* and dig into its archives. A few months earlier, I stumbled across the Internet Public Library, which I had the foresight to bookmark. Finding the Austin newsrag was simple, but it was only archived eight years. A couple of other Austin publications, the *Austin Business Report* and the *Austin Today Monthly* were archived for two and three years respectfully.

Draining my beer, I leaned back and stared at the screen, muttering over the so-called advantages of technology. Here, I'd wasted more time finding nothing than it would have taken me to drive to the library.

I glanced at Jack. "I'm heading over to the PCL at UT," I said, tucking my small notebook in my pocket. "Want anything?"

"The PCL at the UT? What is that?"

I shook my head. "Christ, Jack. You're an uneducated slob for a teacher. You've lived in this town all your life. Don't you know anything? The Perry-Castaneda Library.

It's the main library on the campus, only the fifth largest library in the country."

"Oh." He arched an eyebrow. "Who cares? Just you ex-English teachers. Those of us in coaching have better things to do than read books." He turned back to the TV and ignored me.

"Like what?" I snapped back.

He snorted. "Beavis and Butthead."

"That figures. Morons for morons."

"Get lost."

The library was always crowded. Being an ex-English teacher, I appreciated the intent faces and busy fingers as students scribbled notes. The kind of individual you find in a library is seldom the kind with whom I had to deal in my present business. Restores your faith in the human race. And then you run into a Ted Bundy, or Dean Corell, or Wayne Williams Jr.

I'd been in the PCL often, and I still knew the process even though technology was changing it. Now, all the card catalogues since 1985 were online instead of neatly typed on three-by-five-inch cards arranged alphabetically in hundreds of tiny drawers.

The truth was, I preferred the cards, having researched with that method for the first thirty-odd years of my life.

The microfiche lab was on the first floor. I made my way to the window and requested the 1988 April, May, and June archives for the *Austin Daily Press*.

The library aide, a young college girl who was obviously helping to pay her tuition with the library job, found the cards, slipped me a card to sign, and handed me a white packet containing the microfiche. She indicated the bibliographical data on the front of the envelope. "This is just April . . ." She looked at my name. "Just April, Mr. Boudreaux. We can only issue a month at a time. Are you a student here?"

"No." Aware of the library procedures, I gave her my driver's license. "Just a local."

She gave me a bright smile, and filed my license under the counter. "You know how to use the machines?"

I nodded. "I've been here before."

Half-a-dozen machines that looked like computer screens with an overactive thyroid problem sat back-to-back, three on a side. The square screens were at least twenty inches wide. Four were in use. I took one next to a young man, who parted his black hair in the middle and wore an earring in his bottom lip. Every man to his own poison.

I turned the machine on and slid the square film on the glass carrier. As if by magic, three pages of the *Austin Daily Press* appeared on the screen. April 1, 1988. Taking a deep breath, I moved the pointer to the first page and began scanning, not certain what I was looking for.

Thirty minutes later, I paused and stretched. So far, I hadn't found a glimmer of whatever I was trying to find. I rolled my shoulders, loosening the tight muscles, and returned to the task.

By the time I finished May, 1988, my eyes burned, my neck cramped, and my rear ached. I went back to the window for June, taking my time, trying to work the cricks from my muscles and joints. At least microfiche projectors were almost silent, not clanking and clattering like the old microfilm units.

By ten, with burning eyes and a headache the size of Georgia, I made it through the middle of June, reasoning that Katherine Voss had to have her plans formulated by the fifteenth, the day her father put her on the Greyhound bus. Otherwise, why would she go?

I leaned back and muttered a curse. Nothing. Zilch. *Nada.* "Time to go home to a nice, stiff drink," I grumbled as I slipped back from the projector and headed for the window. Unless. I hesitated in the middle of the floor, recalling the magazine on the table in the visitors' lounge at the distillery.

For a moment, the title eluded me, then I remembered. The *Austin Business Report.* Seconds later, I had the April issue in the projector. The front page jumped out and smacked me between the eyes: BEAUTIFUL BACTERIA BOOMS THE BUSINESS OF BOURBON.

I squinted at the table of contents. I found the article on page 78. The lead paragraph gave me all I needed.

Beatrice Morrison, CEO of Chalk Hills Distillery, announced the discovery of a pure culture yeast, Saccharomyces Cerevisiae, which will create a rich and mellow sour mash bourbon unlike any produced in the United States. The yeast is a vigorous strain that produces its own particular properties for a whiskey that can be distilled to possess various characteristics as desired by the producer.

The article continued, detailing the marketing advantages and financial projections of the discovery. Twice, Alonzo Jackson was quoted, and singled out as the driving force behind the development of the yeast strain, a process that extended over eight years.

"Jesus," I whispered when I finished the article. "Who would have thought anyone could get so excited over yeast?" But then, I reminded myself that people do go nuts over strange things, just like I was going nuts after discovering the reason for Katherine Voss' journey to Chalk Hills.

It was just after midnight when I turned down Travis Street to my apartment. Cars were parked along the curb as usual, creating a one-way street, as usual, and as usual my neighbor's Geo was sticking into the driveway, forcing me, as usual, to swing up on the lawn.

Inside my apartment, Jack snored on the couch. I shook my head. Somehow, I had to get him out of here. I figured he would be gone by now. Maybe he was sore because I didn't pay attention to his monologue and he wanted to get back at me.

A soft knock on the door startled me. I jumped. A knock at the door was the last thing I expected at this time of night. I thought of Jack. "Not another one," I muttered, mentally running down my list of friends whose relationship with their wives resembled the Bosnian war. This was an apartment, not a refuge for battered husbands.

I opened the door a crack, and a sudden force on it propelled me back into the room. "What the—" I yelled, catching my balance and charging back to the door.

I slid to an abrupt halt when a huge shadow stepped inside and the kitchen light revealed his face. Godzilla, alias Huey. He grunted and held the door for Danny O'Banion.

"Get the light, Huey," Danny said softly, stopping in front of me.

Huey closed the door and turned on the light.

Jack mumbled. "Hey, Tony. What's going on here? I was sound asleep. Can't you see—" His words caught in his throat, and he jerked upright when he saw Huey looming over him.

Danny nodded to Jack. "Who's that?"

"Just a friend I'm letting flop here."

"Get 'em out."

Jack's one good eye bulged. "Hey, who—"

"Don't argue, Jack." I snapped at him. "Wait outside."

Huey jerked open the door. "Outside," he growled. "Now."

For a moment, Jack hesitated. "Hey, no one—"

Huey grabbed him by his T-shirt and slung him onto the lawn. "You stay out. You come back when we leave," said the hulking man in his inimitable Neanderthal vernacular.

"You been a busy boy, Tony," said Danny, when Huey closed the door.

I didn't play dumb. I had expected a visit, but not quite so soon. I tried to appear casual. "Yeah. Research. The guy at the distillery getting killed like he did gave me an idea for a mystery."

"A mystery? You mean, like you're writing a book?" He arched an eyebrow in surprise, although a trace of skepticism remained on his face.

"Yeah." I shot a glance at Huey. The way he glared at

me with those wide-set black eyes gave me the feeling that he'd enjoy ripping my arms off.

"I didn't know you was a writer." He eyed me suspiciously.

"Hey, Danny. Every English teacher fancies himself another Shakespeare. One bestseller, and I got it made. The idea of sitting on my tail twenty hours a week and pulling down a couple hundred thousand a year sounds okay to me."

Danny laughed. "I understand that."

"In fact, I even visited a couple of guys at the forensics lab to get some ideas."

Danny glanced at Huey, who nodded.

Just as I figured, Huey had followed me and reported to Danny. "Why?" I gave him a look of pure innocence, of snow-driven purity. "Is something wrong?"

He studied me a moment. "Naw. I just wondered about the extra time you was spending on this thing, Tony. You know, there's nothing wrong with curiosity, as long as it's the right kind. Book writing is the right kind. The wrong kind is unhealthy, you know, like a virus or something. Make a guy sick. Probably even kill him." He grinned and gave me a playful slap on the cheek. "You know?"

I held my hands out to my side. "Look, Danny. I may not be an Einstein, but I'm not stupid. Mrs. Morrison wants me to prove it was an accident. That's what I'm trying to do. You want that, and your . . ." I hesitated, then added, "And everyone wants that. I don't plan on offending nobody."

"So that's what the snooping was all about out at the distillery?"

"Yeah. Research, and trying to find enough evidence for Mrs. Morrison to satisfy her. Besides, Marty doesn't want to turn down four hundred a day either."

He considered my reply for several seconds. I could see the wheels turning in his head as he considered my explanation. "Just be a good boy. You hear?"

I winked at him and held my hand up. "Scout's honor."

He gave Huey a nod, and the gargantuan bodyguard opened the door. Danny winked at me. "See you, Tony."

"Yeah. See you." I hated to lie to Danny, but this was one time the truth would hurt too much.

Huey left the door open, and moments later, Jack scurried inside like a tiny mouse, slammed the door, and gaped at me. His face was drained of blood. Even the yellow bruise had paled. His Adam's apple bobbed like a perch cork. "Wh . . . who was that Frankenstein?"

I shook my head. "You don't want to know, Jack. Believe me, you don't want to know."

The color was returning to his face, and he was getting excited. "Did you see that big thing?" He jabbed a finger at the door. "Did you? That lousy jerk threw me out." Righteous indignation overcame his initial fear. "Why, I should've knocked that big guy on his tail. If he ever lays a hand on me again, I'll—"

"You'll do what he says, Jack. Or you'll end up as part of the interstate."

"Oh, yeah?" His eyes flashed with anger.

"Yeah," I replied matter-of-factly.

He clamped his lips shut and stared at me. I saw the sober realization of my words replace the anger in his eyes. "You're kidding."

"Not on a bet."

Jack stood in his underwear and T-shirt, eyeing me quizzically. Finally, he shook his head and grabbed his pants. "Hey, I'm sorry, Tony. I don't know what kind of trouble you're in, but leave me out." He buttoned his pants, grabbed his shirt, stepped into his shoes, and headed for the door.

"Where you going?"

He stopped at the door and looked back. "To Maggie. I'll take her screeching any day to what you've got here."

I managed to suppress my cheers of joy. "Hey, Jack. You sure? You know, you're welcome anytime."

He hesitated, and for a moment, I thought I'd popped off too soon. The alarmed man shook his head. "Look,

Tony. You need anything, let me know. You're a good friend, but this . . . this stuff . . ." He made a sweeping gesture with his hand. "All this you're tangled up in. I don't understand it, and I don't want no part of it. Okay?"

"Sure, Jack. I understand. No problem. In fact, that's probably the smart thing to do." I hoped I projected the proper degree of dismay and disappointment.

Eager to get away, he fumbled behind him for the door while nodding at the couch. "Just put my stuff in a sack. I'll pick it up later."

I peered between the edge of the blinds and the window as Jack climbed into his car. I waited until he pulled out from the curb and headed down the street before I shouted in joy at the top of my lungs.

My landlady banged on the wall.

Chapter Fifteen

I was exhausted, but too amped by what I had uncovered in the library to sleep. I now had a reason for Voss being in Austin, so to my outline I could add an A.

A. To beg, borrow, or steal the yeast. I didn't have a B, but I decided this one omission could be that occasional exception to grammatical discipline. I tossed some leftover pizza in the microwave and opened a beer. Time to celebrate.

The next morning over coffee, I laid out my day. First, visit Mary Tucker, who claimed she was nowhere near the distillery on Sunday. Even Runnels said she didn't show up. At least, he didn't see her. There was always the possibility she had been there, but kept herself concealed, committed the murder, then vanished, only to reappear two days later. After all, she was a fixture at the distillery, and like janitors and maids—invisible, never seen, and always presumed to be present even when they are not.

But, Tom Seldes claimed he saw her vehicle. Was it hers, or one of the numerous red cars and trucks at the distillery? And who's going to pay attention to a red vehicle coming or going when all the vehicles are the same color?

Personally, I didn't know what was going on, so my next

step would depend on what I found out from Mary Tucker. Then, I would try to get my hands on Claude's ball bat.

By seven o'clock, the temperature had already raced past eighty degrees. A thick haze lay over the city, a choking combination of automobile emissions and an out-of-control forest fire in Mexico. Normally, I drove with the windows down, but the smog was too much for me. I decided to give the air conditioner a try. To my surprise, a weak breath of cool air dribbled into the cab.

During the drive to the distillery, I went over the questions I planned to ask Mary Tucker.

The whine of the forklift came from the open doors of the rackhouse. I paused in the open door and looked around the dark building. Wearing yellow spandex shorts and a green tank-top, Mary Tucker rolled her eyes when she spotted me. She braked the forklift to a halt and removed a soiled gimme cap with a Chalk Hills logo from her head. Her red hair was wet with perspiration. "Christ. I thought we was rid of you."

"Not yet, Mary." I gestured to the floor. "Can we talk a few minutes?"

She tugged the cap on her head. "I'm busy, mister." She ground the gears as she shifted into reverse.

I clenched my teeth against the sudden anger that burned my cheeks. "Fine with me." I shrugged and turned to leave. "But, I imagine you'll talk to the police, and they won't be as easy as me." I headed for the door.

The gears clashed again, and the engine wound down. "Hey, what are you talking about?"

Grinning to myself, I spun on my heel and blasted her with a dose of her own venom. "Look, Mary. I don't care if you talk to me or not, but I kid you not, you're going to talk to someone. You've made no secret of how you felt about Emmett because of what he did to your daughter. I can't say I blame you, but if he was murdered, you've got as good a motive as anyone and better than most. Now, talk to me, and maybe I can keep you out of trouble."

Her florid face grew stubborn. "I ain't in no trouble." Her large nostrils flared, and she clambered down from the forklift.

Some people won't listen until you talk their language. "Don't be so stupid. You got trouble out the ying-yang. Cops find out about your daughter, and you'll be sharing a cell with the kind of ladies you don't want to share a cell with."

She glared defiantly at me, her red-rimmed eyes looking like two buckets of blood against her blotchy skin. Her fists were jammed against her ample hips that bulged the spandex in ways it wasn't designed to be bulged. "I wasn't around here Sunday. I can prove it."

"That's all I'm asking. You tell me where you were, and I'll verify it. If you're telling the truth, you got nothing to worry about." I paused, then added, "All I'm trying to do is pinpoint the whereabouts of anyone who might have wanted Patterson dead. That's all."

For several seconds, she studied me. I could see the wheels turning in her head, slowly, but still turning. Her lifestyle down on Sixth Street wasn't conducive to the salubrious nourishment of brain cells, so it took some time for the few remaining cells to throw themselves into gear.

She glanced around the rackhouse. No one was around, but she lowered her voice nevertheless. I guess she thought a soft tone was appropriate to the revelation of a secret. She stepped toward me and ducked her head. She was close enough that I caught a rank whiff of unwashed flesh. "Look. I tell you something, you keep it to yourself, right? I mean, if it proves I wasn't around here when Emmett got killed?"

I took a step back for a breath of air. It was diesel, but that was better than the odor she gave off. "Yeah. Nobody but me. That's what I've been hired to do, Mary. Prove it was an accident. If I can make sure everyone has an alibi, then Mrs. Morrison will be satisfied that his death was an accident."

"Okay. But, you got to promise not to say nothing to

nobody. I didn't do nothing to Emmett. I woulda liked to. But, I can get in bad trouble if you tell anyone what I say."

I was growing impatient. "Look, Mary. Either spit out what you got to say or I'm leaving. I'm tired of you jacking me around."

The blotches on her puffy face stood out against her pale flesh. "You can't say nothing to Rue or the boys. You got to promise that."

"Rue?"

"Yeah. You remember. Down at the Red Grasshopper. The guy with the tattoos on his arms. He'd hurt me bad if he knew what I'm going to tell you."

"Oh, that Rue." I arched an eyebrow. You can bet I remembered him and his Neanderthal buddies. "Don't worry. Last thing I plan on doing is elbowing up to the bar with Rue and his sidekicks for a beer."

She looked around again. "Okay. I was down in Bastrop on Sunday. Spent the day with a guy named Gus."

"Gus who?"

She grinned crookedly. "Hey, I don't know. Ran into him on Saturday night at a bar. We went back to his place. Stayed there 'til Monday noon."

Jesus, I thought to myself. What was this Gus like to hit the sheets with Mary Tucker? "Where can I find Gus?"

"All I know is he lives on the river. I was pretty drunk when we went there."

I shook my head. "Christ, Mary. How did you know he wasn't some kind of lunatic or something? That's crazy, going with some guy you just picked up."

She looked up into my eyes. A wry grin curled her thin lips that quivered as her brows knit in pain. In a trembling voice, she replied, "Look at me, mister. Look at me good. That answer your question?"

Suddenly, I felt sorry for her. I didn't know what to say, so I fell back on my PI skills. I asked a question. "How can I find Gus?"

"At the Riverside Club. Everyone knows him."

* * *

Leaving Mary in the rackhouse, I climbed in my pickup. I wanted to look in Claude's cabin, but officially, I couldn't. Burglary was the legal name of what I had in mind. Three elements determined burglary; breaking and entering, dwelling belongs to another, and intent to commit crime.

I reasoned that maybe this would not exactly be burglary. After all, there was no intent to commit a crime. I was splitting hairs, but I really wanted that baseball bat.

I studied his cabin, idly watching a calico cat grooming herself on the stack of firewood beside his apartment. My best bet was to return after he got off work. Come up with some lie to get the ball bat.

I glanced around the premises. No one was moving. Why not take a chance? Casually, I knocked on his door. No answer. Good. Despite the fact my heart was thudding against my chest, I moved without haste. I opened the door, stuck my head in, and yelled, giving the impression to anyone watching that I was innocently searching for Claude.

The bat rested on the gun rack not ten feet away. I stepped inside, grabbed the bat and jammed it under my belt, sliding the handle down to my calf and sticking the bleached barrel under my jacket.

Then, as casually as I broke in, I left, walking somewhat stiff-legged back to my pickup, at the same time giving an indifferent glance around the farm. To my relief, no one was storming toward me.

Just for a touch of the dramatic, I paused at the open door of my Chevy and wiped my forehead. Then I climbed into the pickup and slowly drove away, trying to sort my thoughts about Claude. If the bat had bloodstains, I was going to have a hard time tying Claude in as the blackmail victim. I didn't know how much Patterson had demanded, but his possessions indicated a great deal more than Claude could afford.

Another idea hit me. Maybe the blackmail victim paid Claude to whack Emmett. I considered the possibility, then shook my head. No one in his right mind would trust Claude to keep quiet about something like that.

My next move was to find Gus at the Riverside Club, which, to no one's surprise, turned out to be on the bank of the Colorado River in downtown Bastrop.

Finding Gus was no problem. Making sense of his mumbling was another matter. I spent ten minutes at his table and learned nothing.

The owner of the club shook his head when I bellied up to the bar. "You ain't gonna get no sense from that old rummy, mister."

I glanced across the darkened room at Gus, who sat at a corner table muttering to the can of beer before him. "It's only ten o'clock. How many beers has he had?"

"That's his first. The old man comes in, takes two sips and he's drunker'n a skunk. I've knowed a lot of alkies like that. Lose their tolerance, I suppose."

The owner must have read my mind, for he added, "But he don't hurt nothing in here. Everybody knows him. He just sits from morning 'til night. Puts away ten or twelve cans."

I thought about my own drinking. It wasn't excessive, but then maybe neither was Gus' at the beginning. I shrugged the thought off. "Tell me. Last Saturday night. You notice him and a heavy-set woman with red hair?"

He eyed me warily. "You a cop?"

"Private investigator. Just trying to pin down the whereabouts of the woman I mentioned."

He shrugged. "Well, can't help. And that's the truth. Saturday is our big night. Like the old boy said, I stay busier than a callgirl at a political convention."

I studied Gus, then asked, "What about last Sunday? Was Gus here last Sunday?"

"You sure you ain't a cop?"

"Swear on a stack of Bibles." I held up my hand.

He wrinkled his forehead in concentration. "Can't say for sure. He's here all the time, you know. But, now that you mention it, I don't remember seeing him Sunday. He mighta been here, but I can't say for sure."

"Anybody else work here besides you?"

He chuckled and wiped down the bar. "I wish. No, I open this dump and close it, seven days a week. You wouldn't be interested in buying a going proposition, would you?"

It was my turn to chuckle. "No, thanks." So much for Mary's alibi.

On the way back to Austin, I considered my next move. Mary was still suspect. She fit in with the ME tech's conjecture of a woman assailant, and there was no definite proof she spent Sunday with Gus. But, I reminded myself, there was a Gus. She had not invented him. And that lent some credence to her alibi.

Suppose she was the killer. She could have whacked Emmett on the head. But, as fat as she was, how could she leap from a moving tractor, keep her balance, and outrun the discs? Watching the traffic ahead of me, I muttered, "She's so fat, she'd bust her ankles if she jumped off a chair."

On the other hand, she could be a lot stronger than she looked. Manhandling all the barrels up on the forklift took some muscle.

Sometimes ideas grow slowly in your head. Sometimes, they suddenly appear. One second, you're blank, the next, there it is. That's how it happened to me. One moment, I was puzzling over how she could escape the discs, the next second, I knew.

"Dummy," I growled, pounding my forehead with the heel of my hand. "Why didn't you see it sooner?"

The oak. That's how the killer pulled it off. When the tractor went under the oak, all the killer had to do was deliver the blow, throw the club away, grab a limb and hold on until the discs passed under him, or her. Even fat Mary Tucker could have managed dangling for ten or fifteen seconds.

"I'll be," I muttered excitedly. "That's it. That's . . ." A thought stopped me. If the killer had thrown the club away, where did it go? The crime scene boys scoured the area. They found nothing.

The blaring of a horn jerked me back to the present. "What the . . ." I had crossed the yellow line. The leering grin of a Peterbilt grill filled the windshield. I yanked the wheel hard to the right. Tires squealed, and I was thrown against the door as I swerved just in time to miss a head-on with the loaded eighteen-wheeler.

Behind me, horns blared. Speeding vehicles braked to miss me as I careened across two lanes of traffic. The pickup skidded off the macadam onto the graveled shoulder. I hit the brakes and fought for control in white clouds of billowing dust. The pickup hurtled pell-mell toward an unyielding fence of concrete blocks. I felt the brake pedal banging against my foot. I slid to a halt only inches from the fence.

I gulped, and for several moments sat motionless. Finally, I drew a shaky hand across my dry lips. I muttered a soft curse. "That was too close," I whispered.

Slowly, I pulled back onto the shoulder, letting traffic pass until I could move into the outside lane and drive on into Austin at forty miles an hour.

Despite puzzling over the whereabouts of the murder weapon, the excitement of discovering how the killer escaped the discs overcame the chilling awareness of my close encounter with the graveyard. Seems like Runnels had made a remark about seeing the discs under the large oak.

I couldn't remember, and caught up in the midst of the heavy traffic, I wasn't about to sneak a look at my notes. I vowed that could wait until I reached home at forty miles an hour.

So much for vows. Within a few miles, I was tooling along at seventy-five with the other idiots, letting my mind wander right along with theirs, except mine was wandering through the evidence I had slowly compiled, while they dreamed of the coming weekend.

Chapter Sixteen

To my surprise, the black Lexus was nowhere in sight when I turned into the drive. I glanced around, wondering if Danny had pulled the wolves off. That wasn't like him. In school, he never took chances, and I assumed for him to have lived so long in his particular business, he still didn't. He was a great believer in information, and he pulled every string he could when he needed some.

I slipped the bat under my belt and climbed out of the pickup. As I opened the apartment door, I heard the gentle squeak of tires against the curb. I looked around as Huey dropped the Lexus into park, and stared at me over the top of the partially lowered window. I grinned at him, but his rock-hard face didn't flinch.

Once inside, I stuck the bat in the corner of the bedroom closet until I could scrounge up a can of luminol and an ultraviolet light from my old police buddy, Joe Ray Burrus. A couple of squirts of spray on the barrel of the bat, stick it under the light, and if there had been blood on it, the bat would glow like ten thousand fireflies down in a Louisiana swamp.

There were a couple of day-old hamburgers in the refrigerator. I popped them in the microwave and opened a beer. I hesitated, remembering Gus. I poured the beer down the drain and searched the refrigerator for a soft drink.

There were none, so I drew a glass of water from the faucet. "Who needs beer?" I muttered with a sense of bravado. "I can do without it."

While the burgers nuked, I called Joe Ray.

"No sweat," he replied in a whisper. "I'll give you a call as soon as I can collect the . . . ah, the gear."

While I ate, I read back through my notes of the interview with David Runnels. "Here it is," I muttered, reading aloud the notes I had taken. "When I stepped outside, the tractor was going past the tree. I didn't see nothing else for a few seconds, and then this dark pile sort of squirted out from the discs."

I leaned back and studied the notes. Nothing about seeing anyone running from the scene. I visualized the layout. Best I could guess, from the spot where his body was found, no one other than a world-class sprinter could have reached the security of the distillery in less than twenty seconds.

Staring at the ceiling, I muttered, "Besides. If someone was hanging from a limb, he couldn't drop until the discs passed. That means, he would drop at the same time Emmett Patterson popped out. And if that was the case, then Runnels would have seen him."

A grimace twisted my lips. "That blows that theory out of the water."

Then I remembered. The trunk of the tree was between the tractor and the maintenance barn where Runnels had stood. What if the trunk was also between Runnels and the killer? Could the killer have seen Runnels and hidden behind the trunk until Runnels went back into the barn?

That didn't sound right. Best I could picture the scene in my mind, if Runnels had seen Patterson squirt out, he also would have seen the killer dangling from the tree limb.

I made a note to check with Runnels again. There were too many unanswered questions.

Disheartened, I spread the pictures of Emmett's cabin on the snack bar and forced myself to study them. Maybe I could find something here. My neat little hanging-from-the-tree theory was slowly sinking into the quagmire of cold reality.

In addition to being a puzzle freak, Patterson was also a western nut. I held up the picture of the set of horns and studied it. They probably cost a few hundred, unless he stole them from somewhere. On the next wall, three prints of western settings hung next to each other, probably seventy-five bucks or so each. Next was his collection of revolvers, rifles, and shotguns. A few thousand dollars there. Above the gun cabinet was the clock, the Texas clock with the Lone Star face.

"No Neiman Marcus bargain there. Maybe Barnum and Bailey Circus." I laughed, noting how the numbers encircled the star. Twelve at the top point. I took another bite of hamburger and observed that the next point was a two. I shook my head. Each point was numbered—twelve, two, four, eight, ten. Jesus, talk about tourist Texana. Straight out of a Stuckey's gift shop.

On the coffee table lay a stack of puzzle magazines beside his push-button telephone. Nothing remarkable there.

The ringing of my telephone interrupted my thoughts. It was Janice. She started off pouting because I hadn't called her. Within the first two or three sentences, she managed to whine, "You just don't care about me anymore."

I rolled my eyes. "You know better than that. I've been busy working for your aunt."

"Too busy for me?" Her voice trembled. "It's been almost a week."

"I'm never too busy for you, Janice. You know that. In fact, I'd planned on giving you a call today." It was a lie, and we both knew it. I continued. "I thought we might have a nice meal at the Old San Francisco Steakhouse and then go out dancing. It's been a few weeks since we've done that."

She giggled. "I'm hungry for some of your gumbo. Shrimp and oyster. You make it better than anyone in Austin."

I muttered a curse. Gumbo takes a couple of hours to

put together. I glanced at the snapshots on the snack bar. With a sigh of resignation, I decided they could wait. "Gumbo it is."

"But, I want to go dancing too. Why don't we have some drinks and dance a little at the club, then go to your place for gumbo?"

I hesitated, recognizing her subtle hint and her none too subtle intent. What the heck, I told myself. Maybe I did need a break. Sometimes a body becomes so involved, he overlooks the obvious. Besides, what would an evening on the town hurt? "Sounds good to me."

Her voice was bubbly. "Great. I'll pick you up at nine. We'll go in my Miata."

After replacing the receiver, I pulled a bag of fresh shrimp and a bag of oysters from the freezer. While they thawed under a stream of hot water, I assembled the remainder of the ingredients and whipped up a chocolate-colored roux—the Louisiana secret of delicious gumbos—jambalayas, and etouffees.

Roux
4 tablespoons flour
2 tablespoons vegetable oil
1 sautéed large onion
Stir CONSTANTLY over flame until
chocolate colored. If it's black, it's burned.
Add 8 cups water to roux
Then add:
Two pounds shrimp (peeled/deveined)
Pint oysters
¼ cup chopped celery
Salt/pepper to taste
Cook for one hour

I turned the gumbo off before it was ready. Another fifteen minutes after we returned, and it would be tasty and steaming hot, ready to be added to a bowl of simmering rice, the result of which would be a full stomach and clear sinuses.

I sniffed the familiar, rich aroma of the gumbo. No cuisine could match Cajun cooking. I licked my lips when I thought of savory stuffed pork roast, delectable chicken and gravy, or sinful pot roast in aspic, all over steaming rice.

The evening was just what I needed, some relaxation after five days of constant work. Despite our differences and her wealth, I usually enjoyed being with Janice, and that night was no different.

After a few drinks and some close-quarter dancing, we returned to my place. Forgetting my earlier resolve, I made us a couple of stiff bourbons, and while I heated the gumbo, she disappeared into the bedroom, returning moments later wearing my robe and nothing underneath.

Needless to say, we gobbled the gumbo hastily, ignoring the splatters on the snack bar. I fed her a shrimp, which she engulfed with her full lips and, with a naughty gleam in her eyes, sucked on the first two joints of my finger.

With a seductive smile, she headed to the bedroom. "Give me a few seconds."

I nodded, hastily shedding my own clothes.

I waited a few seconds after the door closed, then hurried to it. I opened the door and looked at her on the bed.

That's when I froze.

I stared at the digital clock on the nightstand. Three-fourteen. "I don't believe it," I gasped. "I don't believe it. That's it. That's it."

"Tony? What's it?"

"That's it. That's it."

I turned on my heel and hurried into the kitchen, trying to visualize the snapshot of the Texas clock on Patterson's wall. My pulse raced as I pictured the points of the Texas Star in my fevered brain. The top point of the clock was twelve, the next two, the next—

I felt my throat constrict. Emmett Patterson, the puzzle

nut. Could that be it? I fumbled for the kitchen light and grabbed the snapshots. I laid the tip of my finger on the other points. Four, eight, ten.

Fumbling through my notes, I pulled out the set of sixteen numbers: 1210841084284212. I jumped up and slammed my fist on the snack bar. "Son of . . . that's it. The combination is set up by the numbers on the points of the clock."

I scrabbled through the papers on the snack bar for a pencil and started crunching numbers. Typical of his puzzle fetish, Patterson had left one neat little conundrum.

Janice, a sheet wrapped about her, stormed into the kitchen, her short brown hair mussed, her face flushed, and her lips puffy with unfulfilled passion. "Tony, what is going on?" She stomped her foot.

"Just a minute." I held up my hand to silence her.

If I had paid attention, I would have seen the shock on her face. That I should forego her physical pleasures for a handful of snapshots was beyond her comprehension.

But, typically, I paid no attention. I continued scribbling, hastily sketching out the clock to find the lost numbers. After several seconds of stunned disbelief, she spun on her heel and stomped back to the bedroom, slamming the door behind her.

I ignored her.

The landlady banged on the wall.

I ignored her too.

Emmett Patterson must have had a poor memory to set up such a puzzle as a reminder. Once you figured out the delivery of the numbers, the remaining sets were simple. Beginning with twelve, he counted off the next three points of the star counter-clockwise. Each succeeding set, he began with the preceding point on the star. I reread the numbers in my notes: 12, 10, 8, 4, then 10, 8, 4, 2, then 8, 4, 2, 12.

Now, all I needed was the next logical set of numbers, the set I hoped was the combination of the safe. I jotted them on the slip of paper: 4, 2, 12, 10.

Outside, a horn honked.

The bedroom door slammed. I looked up, and Janice, her clothing askew, glared at me. "That's my cab. I'm getting out of this place." She stormed across the kitchen, slammed a lid on the remainder of the gumbo, cradled it in her arm, and murderously eyed me up and down. With a toss of her mussed hair, she snapped at me, "Get some clothes on!"

Then, gumbo and all, she left, slamming the door again.

And the landlady banged on the wall.

I continued to ignore her.

Too excited about my discovery to worry about Janice's feelings, I quickly dressed and jumped into the pickup and slammed the door. Pulling on the street, I glanced into the rearview mirror. Two headlights pulled out behind me. Huey the Faithful. I'd forgotten about him. I cursed loudly. If I drove out to Chalk Hills this time of the morning, Danny O'Banion would know something was up. Reluctantly, I pulled in at the next convenience store and bought some day-old doughnuts and a loaf of bread, and then returned to my apartment. It was four o'clock.

When I reached my apartment, I discovered that in her fury, Janice had forgotten her Miata. I made sure it was locked before I went inside, where, for the next two hours, I stared at the combination, trying to imagine what could possibly be in the safe for Emmett to go to such lengths to protect. I beat a path between the snack bar and the front window, checking on Huey.

One thing I could say for him, no dog was any more faithful to his owner.

Sometimes, a guy who works his tail off gets a break. Not often, but sometimes the gods smile, and they smiled on me. A piece of luck came my way at ten minutes after six. My Old Faithful, Eddie Dyson, called.

"Just got in, Tony. Saw your message. What's up?"

I wish I could say Eddie called me so quickly because he liked me. The truth is, Eddie is the consummate hustler, the transcendent businessman in the world of the flammer, fleecer, and flimflam man. He called because he knew he was going to get a nice piece of jack from me. So, I told him what I needed.

He took my unusual order with the cool aplomb of the professional dipsy-doodle. "Let me doublecheck this, Tony. Beatrice Morrison, William Cleyhorn, Alonzo Jackson, Thomas Seldes, Claude Hawkins, Emmett Patterson, and Mary Tucker. You want financial histories . . . if they have one, right?"

I glanced at the front window. "You got it, Eddie. Any problems?"

He laughed. "This kinda stuff? A snap. Seven big ones is what it'll cost you. You online?"

"Seven? That's kinda steep."

"I got palms to grease, Tony Boy. The price of doing business. Now, you online?"

I hesitated, not understanding the question. "Online? You mean on the web?" What was he asking that for?

"Yeah. The web. The big WWW. What else?"

Uncertain of just where his question was taking us, I replied warily. "Sure. Why?"

"Your e-mail take attachments?"

"Yeah."

"Give me your address. Once I fill your order, I'll e-mail you the information. You got Visa or Discovery?"

"What do you want to know that for?"

He chuckled. "Hey, Tony. I'm a businessman now. All legit. That's the way of the world today. Give me your Visa number, and I'll bill your account for the seven Cs, just like QVC or Time Life."

I hesitated again.

Eddie explained impatiently. "This way, Tony, you and me don't meet. Anyone watching, they don't see nothing. No one sees nothing swap hands. You get what you want, and I get what I want, all in the privacy of your apartment. No cookies for no one to connect us. Simple. You see?"

I saw, and why not? Personally, I couldn't see any difference in buying information from Eddie Dyson Inc. or a

Thomas Kinkade canvas from QVC. I laughed. "Christ, Eddie. Sometimes you truly amaze me."

"Hey. I amaze myself at times. But, you got to stay up with the technology today if you want to be successful. Now, what is it, Visa or Discovery?"

"Visa."

"How long will this take, Eddie?"

He chuckled. "Not long. This is the age of technology."

I stared at the receiver after he hung up. To paraphrase an old maxim, technology makes strange bedfellows. And instead of warily greasing some slimy hand in a dark booth in the local sleaze bar, I would simply wait in the comfort and security of my own home for the goods. This new technology was indeed changing the way people do business.

No sooner did I hang up than the phone rang. It was Marty Blevins. Gone was his usual southern drawl, that lazy, languishing twang. In its place was a demanding and strident screech. "You still on the Morrison business?"

"Yeah. You know I am, Marty. You told me Wednesday to stay with it." I half-grinned, thinking maybe he was tanked up on Gentleman Jack bourbon.

"Yeah? Well, I'm telling you now to back off. Get your lanky rear into the office Monday. I got work for you. A boatload of subpoenas you're gonna serve."

I held my temper. "What the crap's going on, Marty? You . . ."

"I ain't arguing. You be in the office Monday or find yourself another job. You do what I say, or you're fired."

My temper went south. "Listen, you fat . . ."

The whirring buzz of a dead line interrupted me. I glared at the receiver. "You dumb, stupid . . ." I struggled to find the right word to describe Marty Blevins, but considering he was the armpit of the world, words failed me. He was so dumb, if he tried to sniff coke, he'd get ice cubes stuck in his nose.

I resisted the impulse to slam the receiver back in the

saddle. My luck, I'd break it and be out twenty bucks for another.

Usually, I'm a fairly calm person, not given to impulsive reactions. I like to think through a situation. Of course, half the time I think through something, I end up wrong, but still, I consider the matter as carefully as I can.

So, I calmly put coffee on to brew, then calmly brushed my teeth, calmly shaved, and calmly sat at the snack bar with a cup of coffee and tried to figure out what put a burr under Marty Blevins' saddle at six-thirty on a Saturday morning.

Chapter Seventeen

By the time I finished my third cup of coffee, I decided that Danny O'Banion or his bosses had, for whatever reason, contacted Marty. Only the threat of being altered into a biodegradable substance would make Marty give up the four hundred a day Beatrice Morrison was paying.

I muttered to the pictures on the snack bar. "But why?"

The simple conclusion was that someone wanted me to stay away from the distillery. I shook my head. It didn't make sense. Danny must have passed the word that I was backing off the murder angle.

So why put the muscle on Marty?

Suddenly, my brain took one of those all too infrequent giant leaps. Someone put the muscle on Marty because they thought I was snooping too much. Which meant there was something out there that they—whoever *they* were—didn't want anyone to find.

And that meant I was on the right trail. A charge of adrenaline surged through my veins. I leaned back on the barstool and stared at the ceiling. "Okay, Marty, you got it. I'll be in bright and early Monday morning. But, this is Saturday, and I've got today and tomorrow, two days."

A sharp knock on the door interrupted my thoughts. It was Joe Ray. He pushed inside, carrying a small bag. "I got the stuff. I didn't call. I just came on over after my shift."

My heart thudded against my chest. Now we would see if the bat was the murder weapon. I nodded to the snack bar. "Get some coffee. I'll get the bat."

Moments later I laid the bat on the snack bar. Joe Ray pulled out a can of luminol and sprayed a liberal coat of the liquid on the bat. He plugged in the hand-held ultraviolet light. "Okay. Close the blinds and turn out the lights."

My hands trembled with excitement. If the bat was the murder weapon, that would point to Claude as the killer. I grimaced. There was no way I could figure him being the perp. No way. But, I had to know. I snapped off the kitchen light and turned to the snack bar, expecting to see a bright yellow fluorescent glow.

Nothing.

I glanced at Joe Ray. "Is it dark enough in here?"

"Yeah, it's dark enough. See for yourself. No blood on this baby, Tony." He hesitated, chuckled. "I guess I should have said, don't see for yourself."

With a mixture of disappointment and relief, I flipped the light switch. "Thanks anyway, Joe Ray."

He shrugged and placed the items in his bag. "What's it all about?" He poured some coffee.

I grinned crookedly. "A long story, and it's one of those you don't need to know. A case of better off not knowing."

He arched an eyebrow and sipped his coffee. "Then, don't tell me."

"Thanks. I owe you."

I stood at the door as Joe Ray drove away. I hesitated, glancing up and down the street. I blinked and looked again. Then I stepped out on the small porch and peered up and down the street again.

Huey was nowhere around.

One of my favorite lines in *Julius Caesar* is Brutus' observation, "There is a tide in the affairs of men, which, taken at the flood, leads on to fortune. Omitted, all the voyage of their life is bound in shallows and in miseries."

To translate 17th century dialogue to the vernacular of the 20th century, jump when you get the chance.

I jumped.

Grabbing my notes, the snapshots, and my scribbling, I hurried outside and hopped in my pickup. The tires squealed as I sped south on Travis, taking the first corner on two wheels, expecting at any moment to see the leering front end of the black Lexus pulling in behind me. I took the next four corners the same way until I crossed 360 and hit Bee Tree Road.

Once on the winding road through the limestone hills outside of Austin, I breathed easier. Traffic was light, but I kept a close watch on the rear. No sign of the Lexus, which puzzled me. Huey was too faithful to blow his job. Using my questionable powers of deduction, I decided Danny, after laying down the law to Marty, had pulled Huey off the job.

The only sign of life at Chalk Hills was a scattering of doves, a circling red-tailed hawk, and a few darting sparrows. I drove straight to Patterson's cabin, noticing that same calico cat grooming herself on the stack of firewood against his house.

Without looking left or right, I entered the cabin, flipped on the light, and locked the door behind me. I didn't want to be disturbed. Quickly, I slid the gun cabinet from the wall and gave the dial a spin.

"All right," I whispered. "Let's see if you got it right now, Tony. Right four, then left two." Quickly I dialed in the remaining numbers—one, two, one, and zero.

Nothing.

I dialed again, this time starting left.

Still nothing.

I sat back on my haunches and stared at the dial and then at the numbers on the scrap of paper. A sense of frustration welled in my chest. This had to be the combination. "Uh, oh." I spotted another combination in the set of numbers. The one, two, one, zero could be twelve and ten.

My heart thudded in my chest. I licked my dry lips, gave the dial a spin and then started right four, left two, right twelve, left ten. I thought I heard a click, but my heart was beating so loud, I couldn't be sure.

Gingerly, I tugged at the handle.

The top came off.

I suppressed a shout of triumph.

Suddenly, someone knocked on the door.

Christ! I glanced at the door, then peered into the safe. There was a single envelope. Quickly, I stuffed it in my shirt pocket, dropped the lid back on the safe, and slid the gun cabinet against the wall as the knocking started again.

"Hey! What's going on in there? Open the door!" I recognized David Runnels' gravelly voice.

"Just a minute!" I shouted, hurrying to the door. I made a show of studying the knob when I opened the door. "Look at that. It locked itself. Wonder how that happened?"

Runnels remained in the open doorway. He frowned. "What's going on?"

"Oh, hi. What's up?" I played the innocent.

"What was the door locked for?" He eyed me suspiciously, then glanced at my chest.

"Beats me." I shrugged. "I came out to look around one more time before I give Mrs. Morrison my last report. The door locked on me." I looked around the room, hoping my nonchalance would temper his suspicion. "You might need to check it."

From the corner of my eye, I saw him studying the room.

I turned to him. "Did you need something from me, Mr. Runnels?"

He looked at my chest again, then met my eyes. "Huh? Oh, no. I saw you come in, and I just wondered what was going on."

I glanced down. My heart pounded when I spotted the envelope sticking out of my shirt pocket. I tried to ignore it. "Good. Saves me coming over to see you. I had another question. About last Sunday." I pulled my notebook from my shirt pocket and casually shoved the envelope snugly into my pocket. "You said you stepped outside just as the tractor passed the tree. I think you said that it was a few seconds later that you spotted Patterson. Right?"

He shrugged and cleared his throat. "Yeah. When I stepped outside, the tractor was going past the tree. Like I told you, I didn't see nothing else for a few seconds, and then this dark pile sort of squirted out from the discs."

I held my breath, hoping he had seen someone dangling from the tree or racing to the distillery. "You see anyone else out there? Maybe hanging from the tree."

"Hanging from the tree? What the Sam Hill for?"

"I'm just asking. Did you?"

"No. Not a soul. Why?"

I grimaced. I was missing something. "You sure you saw no one running to the distillery?"

His forehead wrinkled in a frown. "I told you. I didn't see nobody. You want me to write it down for you on that little notebook? What else do you want?"

"One more question. Did you go back into the barn before Mrs. Morrison showed up?"

He frowned. "No. I stood where I was, and when I saw Mrs. Morrison come out of the distillery, I went to meet her."

I tried not to frown. "Thanks, Mr. Runnels." He remained fixed in the doorway. I turned sideways and edged past him. "Excuse me. I'm finished here. I've seen all I need to see."

Back in the pickup, I rethought my theory of the murder. If Patterson was murdered—and at that moment I was willing to bet every cent I had that he was—how did the killer vanish? From the time the poor slob fell from the tractor until the discs passed over him couldn't have taken more than twenty seconds.

Runnels saw the tractor just as it passed the tree. A few

seconds later, he spotted Patterson. And then he saw Morrison come out of the distillery. The killer had nowhere to run. Morrison on one side, Runnels on the other. So how did the killer simply vanish?

With a shake of my head, I shifted the truck into gear and headed back to Austin. As I topped the hill above the distillery, I glanced back. Runnels stood outside the maintenance barn watching after me.

In my disappointment, I'd forgotten the envelope. Now, I yanked it from my pocket and fumbled to open it while trying to stay on the narrow road. I ran onto the shoulder three times, but finally, I ripped the end from the envelope. Several snapshots fell into my lap and spilled to the floorboard.

I muttered a curse and slid the truck to a halt on the graveled shoulder. Quickly, I retrieved the snapshots.

My eyes bulged. "I don't believe it," I muttered, my numbed brain trying to absorb the reality of the images.

Slowly, I viewed the others, five in all. All framed the same two individuals—Beatrice Morrison and Thomas Seldes—naked as the day they were born, and in a variety of positions.

The rackhouse supervisor and the owner of the distillery. I shook my head. Unbelievable. The pictures were old— nine years, according to the date on the back.

Suddenly, everything fell into place. Now, I had a motive, a dandy motive. But, who was Patterson blackmailing, Morrison or Seldes? I shook my head. It had to be Seldes.

But what could have set the muscular man off? What reason could he have had for going ballistic and killing Patterson? I hesitated. There was a flaw in my theory. And not a tiny one either.

When the victim killed his blackmailer, he either had the incriminating documents in his hand, or knew how to put his hands on them. Had Seldes destroyed what he thought was the only set of pictures, not realizing Patterson had another set? That was the only logical explanation. On the other hand, surely Patterson was smart enough to warn Seldes there were extra copies.

I slid the snapshots back into the envelope, but they jammed on something.

I peered inside. There was another scrap of folded paper. I opened it and exploded in curses. "You dirty, no-good— Emmett Patterson, you—" The words stuck in my throat. I stared at another set of cryptic numbers: 2-91-147878969632.

I jammed the paper back into the envelope with the pictures. "Not now," I growled. "I don't have the time for another stinking puzzle."

Shifting into gear and turning on the air conditioner— which decided to function—I pulled back on the road, trying to build a case against Thomas Seldes. But the new set of numbers played mind games with me.

Regardless of the incriminating pictures, there were two pieces of evidence contradicting my theory. First, the assumed blow to Patterson's head was, according to the ME technicians, most likely delivered by a woman. And second, why would Seldes have murdered Patterson without the absolute certainty that he had all the damaging pictures in his possession?

I chewed on my lip. My nice little theory suffered from a few holes. But not as many as Eddie Dyson punched in it when I reached home.

When Eddie Dyson said fast, he meant fast.

In a fourteen page attachment to my e-mail, Eddie provided a detailed financial history of those names I had given him; not only balances in accounts, but for those participating, a history of market trading for the last two years.

I ran down the screen to Emmett Patterson.

I studied his banking history. He had opened his account nine years before, in 1989. He religiously deposited his weekly paychecks in the amount of $374.91. In addition, for the first two years, there were also regular cash deposits in the amount of $500 a month, obviously his blackmail payoff.

The paychecks increased in total about ten percent a year. Not so the blackmail payoffs. They jumped from $500 to $1,000, then $2,000. For the last three years, he had been depositing $5,000 a month, a total of $240,000. I shook my head. A consummate example of pure, unadulterated greed.

Fumbling, I pulled out the snapshots and checked the date on the back again: 1989. Nine years.

Bingo.

Another strike against Thomas Seldes.

I searched the attachment for Seldes' banking history. I expected to see a bare bank balance. To my surprise, Seldes had a twenty-thousand-dollar balance, plus mutuals and stocks worth another four hundred thousand. Going on half a million. And none of Patterson's deposits matched any of Seldes' withdrawals. I winced. That was the bank account of a blackmail victim? Not quite.

Unless, Seldes got his money elsewhere. Maybe Beatrice Morrison?

I shook my head. That didn't feel right. I swallowed the sudden tightness in my throat. Was I wrong? Had I screwed up again?

Morrison's account gave no indication of monthly pay-outs of $5,000 over the last two years. Of course, I hadn't expected any. Someone in her position had no problems in laundering funds in whatever manner or amount she chose.

Hawkins and Tucker lived from paycheck to paycheck.

Jackson, to my surprise, had less than five thousand in his account, but another twelve in savings, forty-three in CDs, and almost thirty in various stocks. I studied his situation, trying to match Patterson's deposits to Alonzo Jackson's withdrawals. Nothing matched.

Seemed like Jackson should have more assets after three decades at an above-average salary. I shrugged, remembering the two girls in the white Mercedes. With a wife and two daughters like those two, the lifespan of a dollar in the

Jackson family probably ran a close race with that of the male Black Widow.

And then William Cleyhorn. Like most attorneys, he had a fat bank account and a portfolio of stocks, blue chips and to my surprise, option trading, a record of calls on Chalk Hills. I grinned. At least, he was loyal while he made money.

Then I caught my breath. Only two weeks earlier, he had purchased contracts of July 100 puts for two hundred thousand on Chalk Hills. Why puts? Another puzzle. Another round hole for a square block. Puts were negative investments, a bet that the value of a particular stock would fall.

I studied the financial report. Why would Cleyhorn work to increase the value of the stock and then turn around and spend two hundred grand on a gamble that the stock would drop? I studied the report. I couldn't tell if he'd bought one or two contracts.

There was something rotten somewhere. And Denmark was a heck of a long ways from Austin, Texas.

From what little experience I had with the market, I knew players of the options, calls and puts, were gambling big time with God, but there were many investors who did have a portfolio of stocks on which they bought options as a hedge against rising and falling values.

While the printer spit out a hard copy of the attachment, I studied the screen. I couldn't help admiring Eddie Dyson's speed and thoroughness. A true entrepreneur. Find a marketing niche and fill it. In his case, however, I didn't want to know how he managed to gather his data.

My next step was to revisit Thomas Seldes. I was curious as to his explanation of the snapshots, even though his financial assets did not indicate blackmail payments, certainly not at the rate of $240,000 over three years. Still, considering the pictures, he was my first choice.

And if I wasn't satisfied with him, Beatrice Morrison would be next.

* * *

On the way back to the distillery, I pulled in at a Stop N' Go and placed the pictures side-by-side on a copier, printing them onto a single page. Then I placed the originals in a self-addressed envelope and dropped it in the mail to me.

During the thirty-minute drive to the distillery, I toyed with Emmett Patterson's new puzzle, 2-91-147878969632. After the initial shock of a new puzzle, I immediately recognized the first three digits, the rackhouse and the year the bourbon was put up to age. And if he followed suit, then the key to the remainder of the riddle was in his apartment. After solving his last puzzle, I believed I knew where to look.

I slowed at the crest of the hill overlooking the distillery. I had the distinct feeling that the entire case was coming to a head, and yet, if I had to place a bet on the nose of the killer, I couldn't do it. Seldes seemed the logical one, but there was no evidence he had paid any blackmail. There was no evidence anyone paid blackmail. Yet, what was Emmett Patterson doing with the pictures?

He was blackmailing someone. His lifestyle and his income didn't match. He had to have another source of income.

Chapter Eighteen

I stopped at Patterson's cabin first. Leaving my pickup running, I ducked inside and checked his telephone. It was pushbutton as I expected. That was the key. I couldn't resist a smug grin as I returned to my truck. Eat your heart out, Sherlock Holmes.

It was a slow day in the rackhouse. The heat rose from the ground in debilitating waves, thick enough to suck the breath from your lungs.

Initially, I'd wondered why the rackhouses weren't air conditioned, but Seldes had explained that the heating and cooling process forced the aging alcohol in and out of the charred wood inside the barrel, imparting a delicate, subtle flavor.

From the rear of the huge barn came the whine of the forklift. Seldes was talking on the telephone when I entered the double doors. He glanced at me and nodded.

I studied him while I waited. He wore his usual khaki attire. If I hadn't seen the pictures, no amount of arguing could have convinced me that he and Beatrice Morrison had a fling. Beauty and the beast all over again.

With a jerk of his head, he spoke sharply into the receiver, then put it down with a bang. He grinned sheepishly at me when he realized I witnessed his behavior. "Sorry.

Those guys at the Round Rock rackhouse. If you're not there to hold their hands, they can't get nothing done." He continued in his high-pitched voice. "Now, what can I do for you, Mr. Boudreaux. You oughtta about be finished with your investigation. It's been almost a week."

Arching an eyebrow, I shrugged. "I think I am about finished. Just a couple more questions. Some that I figure you'll have the answer for." I watched him carefully, but he gave no indication of any alarm or concern.

He chuckled. "Well, I'll do my best. But the truth is, I can't tell you anything more than I did the other day. I wish I could."

"Oh, I think you can this time, Mr. Seldes." I glanced around the rackhouse. We were by ourselves. I decided to push him hard. "Emmett Patterson was blackmailing someone. I couldn't figure out who, and then I found some pictures he kept in a safe."

He frowned, obviously puzzled. "Pictures?"

I unfolded the sheet of paper on which I had copied the pictures and handed it to him. I took a step back, and waited, wondering if he was going to bolt.

His jaw dropped, his eyes grew wide. He tried to speak, but the words clogged in his throat. He staggered back. His knees seemed to wobble, and he leaned against the wall to keep from falling. "My God," he mumbled. "My God." He looked at me in disbelief. "W . . . where . . . where . . ."

I answered his question tersely. "Patterson."

He shook his head, trying to clear the confusion. "But . . . but how did . . ." His words died in his throat.

"This is you and Mrs. Morrison, isn't it?" Without giving him time to reply, I continued. "That's about the best blackmail material I've seen in a good while. Now, what about it?"

He removed his hat. Sweat beaded on his pale forehead and ran down his face. "Do . . . do you mind if we go up to my office? It's . . . it's cooler up there. I . . . I'm feeling kind of funny."

I eyed him warily. "After you." I followed him up the

stairs, his broad shoulders slumped forward, his bowed legs moving slowly. I remained a few steps behind, just in case he decided to make a break. I might not be able to stop him, but I could sure slow him down.

In his office, he sagged into the chair behind his desk and stared at the sheet of pictures. He shook his head. "I can't believe it."

I closed the door behind me and remained standing. "Tell me about the pictures."

The older man looked up at me, his eyes filled with pain, his face twisted with anguish. "What's to tell? You've seen them."

"How much did you pay Patterson to keep quiet?"

"Pay?" He knit his brows, as if uncertain of my meaning. "Emmett? Pay Emmett Patterson?" Then he nodded slowly when he understood my question. "Nothing. Why, I never knew he even had these pictures."

It was my jaw that dropped open then. "You mean, he never approached you with these pictures?" I found that response difficult to believe. Difficult? How about impossible?

Seldes' face grew firm with resolve. "I can't . . . deny the pictures, but no, Emmett Patterson never approached me about them. I never paid him a cent in blackmail money. Or any other way," he added steadfastly, resting his elbows on his desk and leaning toward me.

"Why should I believe you?"

He eyed me. I figured he was weighing just how much he should say. "Look, I've worked for Chalk Hills fifty years. Joe Morrison hired me when I was a kid. I've never made more than forty thousand a year, and that much only in the last eight or ten. I started out at thirty a week. I've got no family except the people out here. I have about twenty thousand in the bank and close to four hundred thousand in mutuals and stocks. There ain't no way I could have accumulated that much and paid a jerk like Emmett Patterson blackmail." He held the sheet of pictures up. "Especially if these was what he was using on me. The truth of the matter is, if he was using these, he could have got a lot more from Beatrice than me. But he didn't. It's the God's truth. I didn't know the slimy creep had these pictures."

"Maybe she was the one he was blackmailing."

Seldes eyed me a moment. He shook his head. "No. I would have known."

It was my turn to arch an eyebrow. "Oh?"

"Yeah."

A pathological liar can easily tell any story with enough conviction and sincerity to convince even the most skeptical. Either Tom Seldes was a master of body language, or he was telling the truth. There were none of the signs of lying, or nervousness; no looking away, no fidgeting.

He didn't strike me as a liar. And he was right. Chalk Hills was his life. I had the feeling he never went anywhere, did anything, and purchased any item unless it had to do with the distillery. Probably his biggest expense was a few sets of khaki suits each year. What did he have to lie about? The number of khaki suits he bought? His accumulation of assets despite a not-too-impressive salary was testimony enough that he did no excessive spending.

"What about the pictures?"

He knit his eyebrows in pain. With a sigh, he shook his head and began in a soft, thin voice. "Years ago, almost thirty-five, Beatrice and me had a few dates, halfway serious, but when she met Joe Morrison, that was it. He was twenty years older than her, and he was rich."

I grunted. "Sounds familiar."

"Oh, no. She was a good girl. Her family was dirt poor, and she didn't have much education. So naturally, when someone like Joe showed interest . . ."

"She dropped you."

He grinned feebly. "Suppose you could say that. Anyway, about ten years ago, Beatrice came to my cabin one Sunday when everyone was away. Joe had been dead several years, and she was just lonely, so . . . well, you got the pictures. But, that was the only time. And that's the truth.

And that's why I would know if she was being black-mailed. She would have told me."

I pushed away from the door and sat in the chair across the desk from him. "How do you figure Emmett got the pictures?"

He grew thoughtful. "You know, thinking back that Sunday in my cabin, I had the feeling someone was watching. I never saw anyone or anything. But, I had a feeling. I just marked it off as being nervous about what we were doing."

And I had a feeling, one that was shouting at me that Thomas Seldes had nothing at all to do with the murder of Emmett Patterson. "If you're telling me the truth, then who was he blackmailing?"

Seldes studied me several seconds. "You remember earlier in the week when you first talked to me. You mentioned the fancy clothes, the car."

"Yeah. So?"

"So, that got my attention. I'd kinda wondered about that too. I'd never paid a whole lot of attention, but when you mentioned it, it hit home with me. Made me start wondering if he was dealing in drugs or had something on someone?"

"And? You come up with anything?"

He grinned sheepishly. "No. I wish I could help you out, but I got no idea. No one around here has mentioned nothing about Emmett putting any kind of pressure on them."

I sighed. I believed the man.

That left Cleyhorn and Jackson, the lawyer and the Master Distiller, Emeritus. A well known, highly respected lawyer and a renowned brewer in the World of Whiskey.

Finding a connection was going to be much easier said than done.

Seldes leaned forward. "Do you really believe someone killed Emmett? That it wasn't an accident?"

I thought about Danny and his friends, and the warning I'd been given, so I did the sensible thing. I lied. "No. I just wanted to get to the bottom of this blackmail scheme, that's all. I figure his death was an accident." I hoped Seldes wouldn't pursue the question.

I rose. "I'll hold on to the pictures until this is all over. If what you say is true, if the pictures have nothing to do with the case, I'll give them to you to destroy."

He smiled gratefully and stood, extending his hand. His feet tangled in his chair, which clattered to the floor behind him. He spun, trying to maintain his balance. He threw out his hand for support against the wall, but his arm crumpled on him, sending the muscular man sprawling to the floor.

I hurried around the desk, but he had already sat up and was rubbing his shoulder gingerly. "You okay?"

"Yeah. Yeah." He rose to his feet, continuing to massage his shoulder. "Blasted shoulder joint," he muttered. "Can't take any kind of pressure."

Physically, Tom Seldes looked like he could handle any kind of pressure from anything. "What's wrong with the shoulder?"

"They call it monkey shoulder," he explained, gesturing to his shoulder. "After years of turning barley with a shovel, something happened in the shoulder joint." He held his arm over his head and brought it forward slowly like he was swinging a club. "I don't have any strength like this. I can lift heavy weights, but sometimes, I can barely close a door."

I clicked my tongue. "Monkey shoulder, huh? Seems like Jackson mentioned that once."

"It's a pain in the neck." He grew sober. "What now? You got much more to do to finish up?" He glanced at the sheet of pictures crushed in his hand.

"Just about finished," I lied again, hoping he believed me. I knew that as soon as I left, he'd go straight to Beatrice Morrison. I couldn't afford to blow a hole in my cover story. I reached for the door.

"Mr. Boudreaux. Tony?"

"Yeah." I looked back.

"You believe me?"

I considered his question several seconds. "Yeah. I believe you, Tom."

Another lie. Despite my own feelings, I couldn't afford to believe him, not completely. He could be the world's greatest liar. I had to keep digging and fitting pieces in the puzzle. Sooner or later, it would reveal a picture of the killer.

He started down the stairs ahead of me. "I'm glad," he said.

"One thing, Tom. This little conversation of ours. Let's keep it between us. Neither one of us wants news of these pictures to get out." I hoped the threat of the pictures would keep him quiet. "And Mrs. Morrison certainly doesn't need to know about them. Later, you can do what you want."

He looked up at me a moment, a frown wrinkling his forehead. Then he nodded and lumbered on down the stairs. He still reminded me of a gorilla.

And suddenly, I knew how the killer made his escape. The oak. Christ. How simple. Even Beatrice Morrison could have pulled it off. Unlikely, but very possible. I remembered the face in the window staring down at us, and the Band Aid on Jackson's cheek.

And then, just as abruptly, Seldes was back in the picture. Maybe he had lied, and I'd swallowed it. While I had tentatively eliminated him because the ME techs theorized the blow was not the damaging blow of a man, I now realized the blow could have been struck by a man with a bad shoulder, with a monkey shoulder.

Tom Seldes. No power in his swing. His blow would have the strength of a woman's, and he had the physical strength to effect the escape. On the other hand, I couldn't fit his financial position into the jigsaw puzzle of blackmail.

Back in the pickup, I studied my notes. Sometimes, you have the feeling that you're staring at the answer even though you can't recognize it. Other times, you just stare. I just stared.

I laid my notepad on the seat beside me. "Maybe it'll come to me later," I mumbled, shifting into gear and heading back to Austin.

Chapter Nineteen

I was exhausted from lack of sleep, but I pulled into a convenience store for a six-pack of soft drinks. When I turned down Travis to my apartment and discovered that moron neighbor with the Geo had completely blocked my drive, my temper snapped. I broke into a blistering diatribe of colorful obscenities that didn't even begin to describe the offending driver's genealogy and depleted mental capacity.

The nearest parking slot was in the next block. Grumbling, I wedged the pickup into the space and cursed all the way to his apartment. I pounded on his door. No answer. I pounded again. Still no answer.

Still cursing, I stomped down to my place.

Inside, I pulled the set of numbers from my pocket and checked my theory. I reread the numbers, 2-91-147878969632. I knew the answer to Emmett Patterson's puzzle. I shook my head and muttered. "Now, all I have to do is figure out what it is the answer to."

I opened a soft drink and moved into the living room. The curtains were pulled against the early afternoon sun. The aquarium was a brightly lit rectangle in the midst of the shadows engulfing the room. I stared at Oscar as he continued to swim in circles, never tiring.

"I don't know how you keep it up, Oscar," I muttered,

openly admiring the little guy's dogged determination to keep swimming. "Because, you idiot," I chastised myself, "if he stops swimming, he dies." I imagined his tiny, pink fins halting their rapid motion; his penny-sized body sinking slowly to the sand and gravel; and his belly turning up.

No, Oscar would never stop swimming. He couldn't afford to, just like I couldn't afford to waste a minute. I didn't have time to stand around, guzzle soft drinks, and admire a Tiger Barb's perseverance. Maybe there was something Freudian in my decision to take Oscar at the divorce instead of the TV. Maybe it was because I would soon learn just how stubborn he could be.

Al Grogan might be the most perceptive investigator at Blevins' Investigations, but I was the most stubborn. That trait I picked up early. I was never the best at much of anything, from football to math, especially math. But I was good at stubbornness, at determination.

Day after day, I saw my grandfather go out and farm even when we'd had months of drought. He never quit, and I discovered if I just kept trying, often I could wear down those smarter and stronger than me. Not always, but enough to make it worthwhile.

I hiked my leg over the back of the chair and sat in front of the computer. Booting it, I pulled up the file I bought from Dyson. Quickly, I printed a hard copy of the complete file, then backed it up to another floppy, which I tossed into the desk drawer.

I took the printout to the couch where I could be comfortable. For the next couple of hours, I studied the printout, looking for any logical lead that might point me in the right direction.

I eliminated Morrison and Mary Tucker because I couldn't believe they had the strength or balance to execute the escape. Temporarily, I eliminated Runnels because he was with Morrison when we arrived at the scene. Tom Seldes and Claude Hawkins came up moments later. For any of the three to effect their escape from the scene and return so quickly was improbable, but still possible.

That left Cleyhorn and Jackson.

Neither man's financial records indicated blackmail. Of course, Jackson didn't have the portfolio of Cleyhorn, but on the other hand, Cleyhorn was a lawyer, and Jackson was a distiller. Cleyhorn knew the secrets of how to build a portfolio, even with other people's money, and Jackson had a wife and two daughters who knew the secrets of spending money.

I leaned back and stared at the ceiling, trying to come up with every reason—regardless of how bizarre—that would have given Patterson the leverage to extort money from either Cleyhorn or Jackson.

I drew a blank. I forced my brain to concentrate, despite the fatigue trying to close my eyes.

I gave in to the urge and closed my eyes. Instantly, I fell asleep.

When I awakened an hour later, I was refreshed. I turned back to my task, finding just what leverage Patterson used to extort money from either Cleyhorn or Jackson.

First, Patterson didn't run in the same circles with Jackson or Cleyhorn, so I crossed out social. What was left?

All that was left was business. The distillery. The distillery was the only thing they had in common.

Outside, the sun had dropped behind the hills to the west, and dusk crept over the city like a silent spider. I reached for my notebook, then remembered I'd left it on the seat of my pickup. With a soft curse, I rose from the couch and headed for the door.

I was still cursing the idiot who'd blocked my driveway when I reached my pickup in the next block. Quickly, I retrieved the notebook and headed back.

Just before I came to the end of the block, I spotted a black Chrysler easing slowly down the street in my direction. I hesitated. The hair on the back of my neck bristled. The Chrysler stopped in front of my apartment and three men jumped out, each clutching an automatic with a silencer.

Immediately, I dropped to my knees behind a patch of rose bushes.

The three goons entered my apartment. I crouched lower into the roses.

Moments later, they burst out, one carrying a sheath of papers clutched in his hand. I remained silent, and tried to play the part of a silent little rose bud.

I didn't recognize any of the three, but they were the kind you could find at the bottom of any barrel.

I wedged my body deeper into the rose bushes as the dusk deepened. I knew no one was in my apartment, but perhaps the bozos had placed a lookout somewhere up or down the block.

The dark Chrysler had long since disappeared down the street when I rose from the bushes and hurried back to the apartment.

Someone had put out the word. Seldes? I didn't think so.

Rummaging through my desk, I grabbed the floppy containing the files. I searched for the printout, but it was gone. Then I remembered the sheath of papers one of the goons clutched in his hand.

Quickly, I inserted the disk in the drive and called up the file to print. My printer is a laser, seven pages a minute, but it seemed like an hour before it spit out the fourteen pages.

I eyed the telephone wistfully. "Don't be an idiot," I muttered. "It's got to be bugged." I dropped my Colt .38 in my pocket, and prayed I wouldn't have to use it.

After two hours of driving around Austin, doubling back, speeding up, slowing down, using every trick I knew to ditch a tail, I turned into an exclusive neighborhood near Barton Springs and found a side road from which to spot any tail. Several minutes passed. I breathed easier.

Shifting into gear, I drove through the neighborhood, and wound through several more additions before pulling onto Loop 360 which, after a few miles, turned into Highway 71.

A few miles farther, I took the I-35 cutoff to San Antonio. Fifteen minutes later, after passing all the new commercial hotels and restaurants springing up, I pulled off I-35 just past Leon's Family Steakhouse and parked in the shadows behind a cheap motel local hookers used as a home base, with all the essential amenities of two-hour rent and single-sheet beds.

I paid in advance and hastily retreated to my room, a shabby dump with dirty walls, dirty sheets, and dirty floors. Using the pillowcase, I wiped a layer of dust off the table and brushed several cockroach legs from the chair.

Spreading the printout, my notes, and the pictures of Patterson's room on the greasy table, I tried to build a case against Cleyhorn or Jackson despite the ME technicians' theory that the blow was likely struck by a woman.

For all practical purposes, I had eliminated the others, even Tom Seldes with his monkey shoulder. By going after Cleyhorn or Jackson, I knew I was reaching. And sometimes reaching worked.

Assume Patterson blackmailed Jackson.

Why?

Had the brewer also slept with Beatrice Morrison? If that was the case, why did Patterson hold back the pictures of Seldes and Morrison? Why not blackmail both?

I shook my head. That didn't feel right. So what could it be? I gazed at the drawn blinds on the window. What if Jackson was being blackmailed for something else? What did Jackson and Emmett Patterson have in common?

Scribbling hastily, I jotted a list of everyone involved in the investigation. When I wrote the name, Katherine Voss, I hesitated, then continued the remainder of the list.

But, I was drawn back to Katherine Voss. I read her name aloud. She was the only one on the list unaccounted for. I started playing 'what if.'

The ideas began flowing. I picked up my pencil and jotted down my observations. "Okay. Number one, she's been missing for ten years. Second, she was last seen alive at Chalk Hills. Third, what if something transpired between her and Jackson that Emmett witnessed?" What could Patterson have held over Jackson's head that was worth over a quarter-million in blackmail? Illicit sex? No.

Suddenly, a couple of pieces of the puzzle slid into place. The relatively weak financial status of Alonzo Jackson had bothered me. Such a status could be the result of monthly blackmail. With his income, he should have accumulated more than the ninety thousand or so despite a spendthrift family.

And it could explain why Seldes wasn't being blackmailed. Patterson already had one sucker. Seldes was insurance against the possibility of the first blackmail scheme falling through.

I hesitated. A tenuous idea about the tractor popped into my head, and as abruptly disappeared. I struggled to pull it back. I had the crazy feeling it was the answer to my questions. But try as I might, the idea, the thought, evaded my efforts.

I glanced anxiously at the door. I wanted to talk to Alonzo Jackson, but before I could chance seeing him, I had to find out what kind of tricks Danny was pulling by sending his goons after me.

To accomplish that, I needed a bargaining tool, a reason for Danny and his bosses to back away. But, all I had was a mountain of speculation, a sheath of stolen bank records, and a far-fetched theory. And a theory without the basis of solid facts was not the stuff to make bargaining worthwhile.

Obviously, someone thought I was getting too close to something. That's why the goons showed up. While Danny never admitted Cleyhorn was the one responsible for the first warning, he never denied it. I was convinced Cleyhorn was the contact to whom Danny had earlier alluded.

I focused on Cleyhorn. His financial status was impressive, even for a lawyer. So why was he investing in calls and puts? Next to Russian roulette with five out of six cylinders loaded, playing options is the riskiest investment a man can make. I was no whiz at stocks, having lost money more than once on poor investments. In fact, I'd lost money on calls and puts.

I knew options. I could understand Cleyhorn buying calls. Calls were speculations upon rising stock values, but puts were gambles on falling values. Cleyhorn knew Chalk Hills stock would rise, so his options should have been calls. And some were.

So why would he invest two hundred thousand on the chance Chalk Hills value would drop? Last Sunday, both Morrison and Cleyhorn were concerned the murder would cause prices to plummet, yet a week earlier, he had purchased July 100s. Contracts set to expire at the end of July. Something didn't fit. No sane man invested in puts unless he knew the stock was primed to take a plunge. And a plunge in Chalk Hills stock was nowhere in sight.

I leaned back and stared at his financial records. Ten years earlier, I spent two thousand dollars gambling that the value of TNT Publications would drop. The stock rose, and I was wiped out.

The only way Cleyhorn could come out on this investment was if the value of Chalk Hills dropped. And he was too smart to take that kind of risk based solely on the vagrant caprices of the stock market. He had to know something.

Suddenly, I had my bargaining tool with Danny O'Banion: Cleyhorn's anticipation of Chalk Hills stock dropping. I wondered how Danny's bosses would react to that.

Now, all I had to do was get to Danny before his goons got to me. And I wasn't fooling myself that they wouldn't.

Probably every mutt on the street had a description of my pickup. I'd be fingered before I went a block.

But, it was a chance I had to take. I glanced at my watch. Almost eleven. If I could make downtown Austin, swing off at the Second Street exit, from there I could make it on foot if necessary.

They caught up with me on I-35 just as I passed Ben White Road.

A black Chrysler pulled up on my left and tried to force me off the Interstate. I slammed on the brakes and, as he shot past, I pulled in behind him and accelerated, driving my bumper into the rear of the vehicle. It fishtailed, and the brake lights flashed.

A face appeared in the rear window, then a dark object. I didn't wait to figure out what the object was. I swerved right, cutting through the traffic, heading for the shoulder.

Tires squealed. Horns blared. But I made it across two lanes and bounced over the grass to the access road where I took the first right.

On the Interstate, the Chrysler tried to reach the outside lane, but traffic blocked him in.

I wound through back roads until I reached Riverside Drive, expecting at each corner to run into the Chrysler again. The lights of downtown Austin beckoned. I kept my head and eyes moving, peering into every shadow, every driveway, parking lot, knowing that sooner or later, I'd spot the Chrysler.

We spotted each other just as I pulled onto the access road to the Town Lake Bridge spanning the Colorado River. This time, the Chrysler whipped behind me and pulled up on my right and opened the show with bullets. One punched a hole in my back window. I ducked and swerved at the limo. The goon hanging out the window screamed and jerked his head back in the open window the instant before I slammed into them, knocking them into the concrete barrier.

Metal shrieked. Sparks flew.

Abruptly, I hit the brakes and tried to pull in behind the large car, but the driver had learned his lesson earlier. His brake lights flashed again. I bounced off his front fender.

A line of traffic came up behind us. I cut in front of the upcoming traffic and roared onto I-35, heading for the first exit past the bridge. My old Chevy pickup was no match for the Chrysler on the Interstate.

It was an eerie feeling. They had silencers, and the only way you knew they were firing was the ping of a slug tearing through metal, or popping as it punched a hole in the window.

A thousand thoughts ran through my brain as I sped down the Interstate. Foremost was the fact the gas tank was behind the seat. All it would take was a single slug, and the pickup would balloon into a ball of fire. Such a possibility made priority-setting easy. I was getting out of the truck as fast as I could.

I shot off the freeway and down the Second Street exit to the three-lane access road that had been cut into the side of a steep limestone hill. Ahead, two vehicles stopped for a red light at Cesar Chevez Street.

Without glancing either way, I whipped around them. The Chrysler stayed on my tail. The light at Sixth Street changed as I reached it. Abruptly, the rear end of the pickup whipped crazily to one side. The goons had hit a tire.

I fought for control as I cut across the access road, bounced over a curb and clattered across the parking lot of a Texaco convenience store at the corner of the access road and Seventh Street. Behind the store, a hill rose sharply.

Slamming on the brakes, I leaped from the pickup before it stopped and darted up the sidewalk into an older neighborhood, searching for some dark cubbyhole where I could hide. At the top of the hill, I raced across the street and hurried past the Mercado Jaurez Restaurant.

Dogs barked. A cat darted in front of me. Behind, I heard shouts, and then headlights shot over the crest of the hill. I rounded a corner and dashed into a thick growth of jasmine and bougainvillea.

Seconds later, two dark figures raced past. I waited until the echoes of their footsteps had died away before backtracking. I paused at the corner. Across the street was the Texas State Cemetery, eighteen acres of darkness.

The four-foot fence was wrought steel, each bar about a foot apart. If I could jump it . . . I shot across the street. Just as I reached the fence, sparks flew from one of the steel posts and the whining hum of a ricochet broke the silence.

"There he goes."

I vaulted the fence, snagging my pants on one of the spikes and tumbling headlong to the ground. I leapt to my feet and headed deep into the shadows of the cemetery. I muttered a curse. Of all places to confront Danny's goons. A cemetery. Despite the fear coursing through my veins, I couldn't resist a wry grin at the irony of my situation. At least, they wouldn't have far to go to bury me, or them.

Chapter Twenty

A hundred-and-forty-eight-years-old, the Texas State Cemetery is filled with majestic tombs, greater-than-life statues, and massive headstones, all in various stages of condition. Ancient oaks and pecan trees provided cool shade from the relentless Texas sun during the day, and welcome hiding spots at night.

I paused in the shadows behind a marble crypt and peered into the dark behind me. I had no idea how many soldiers Danny had sent. Three at least. Maybe four.

To the west, the noise and lights of Austin filtered through the thick canopy of limbs and leaves. Danny O'Banion was less than seven blocks away in his office. I grimaced. This wasn't the time for me to confront anyone, especially three or four anyones in a dark cemetery. This was the time to run.

Staying in a crouch, I zigzagged across the graveyard, heading for the west gate. Time dragged. I could hear my pursuit, moving slowly, steadily, and they had separated.

Suddenly, a gravelly voice sounded just to my left. I froze and sunk into a crouch deep in the dark shadows of a headstone. "Any luck?"

A distant voice replied. "Keep looking."

The voice drew closer. I strained my eyes in an effort to pick out substance from shadow. Without warning, a silhouette appeared over me, close enough that I could reach out and touch. I held my breath.

A sharp pain stung my ankle. I had squatted in a bed of fire ants, and the little carnivores were chewing on my ankle. I couldn't budge. Even the slightest movement would sound like a gunshot.

The looming silhouette stood motionless for what seemed like hours. His arm moved, and I heard the unmistakable ripple of a zipper. I doubled my fist, ready to bust him where it hurt most, but he turned his back when he relieved himself.

By now the ants had gravitated up my calf and were proceeding toward my knee, trying to gnaw the flesh from the bone. Sweat dripped from my forehead, but I remained frozen in the shadows.

Then a distant shout sent him in motion. He zipped his pants and finally disappeared into the inky night.

I tried to count to fifty before I moved, all the while trying to push the burning stings from my head. When I hit twenty, I said to heck with it and scrubbed my hand up and down my leg.

Staying in a crouch, I dashed to the next headstone, pausing in the shadows to scratch at the biting ants. By now, my leg was on fire all the way up to my knee. I knelt and pulled up the leg of my jeans. Peering into the darkness around me, I scratched at my leg, smashing the little savages.

Ten minutes later, I ducked into the shadows cast by a large monument, an obelisk mounted on a pyramid, and peered down at the west gate. The Daughters of the Alamo had planted shrubs along the fence years before, and by now, the shrubbery had taken over the fence. If I reached those shadows without being spotted, I could slip across the street and cut through a few backyards, and slide down the hill to the Interstate access road.

There was no traffic on Navasota, the adjacent street, and all the houses facing the cemetery were dark. I glanced over their roofs. The golden glow of streetlights lit several high rises, and the traffic on I-35 was a muted roar.

Moving slowly, I eased toward the gate, every sense alert. I saw nothing, heard nothing. I paused behind an oak several feet from the fence and studied the shadows, searching for any movement.

Finally, I chanced it. On the balls of my feet, I sprinted the short distance separating the tree from the fence and pressed up against the shrubs, rustling the leaves.

"Hey. Who's that?"

The guttural voice froze me. My heart thudded in my chest. I peered into the darkness, trying to make out any movement. Then I heard footsteps on the other side of the fence. They headed for the west gate, which was less than ten feet distant.

Moving slowly, I wedged myself into the shrubs, hoping the shadows would hide me.

The footsteps grew faint, then more pronounced as the goon passed through the gate and headed back toward me. I blinked at the sweat stinging my eyes and flexed my fingers about my Colt.

The crunch of gravel and leaves grew louder. Abruptly, a silhouette, less than two feet away, passed between me and the cemetery. I held my breath.

He continued walking.

My shoulders sagged in relief. I waited a couple of minutes after his footsteps faded into the darkness, and then I slipped past the gate and raced across the street to the first corner and ducked into the shadows.

A dark figure appeared down the block, so I sprinted west on Eighth Street, which ran up and down two steep hills before dead-ending into San Marcos Street.

By the time I reached San Marcos, my lungs were burning, and I was gasping for breath. I hid in the shadows, trying to bring my thumping heart back down from the heart attack range. Across the street were the walls of the French Legation, a Greek revival structure complete with stone walls, constructed in 1839.

The Interstate was two blocks beyond the French Legation. I darted across the street and ducked into a narrow drive that followed the south wall of the historical landmark.

Just as I reached the top of the hill, headlights hit the trees above my head. I dodged into a clump of bougainvillea and waited until the long, black Chrysler slowly passed. Inside the vehicle, the dull glow of dash lights cast a scowling face in stark relief.

I had crouched in the shrubbery between two houses, each with a fenced backyard; one a chain link, the other a stockade. I hated fenced backyards.

Glancing over my shoulder, I spotted the brake lights of the Chrysler at the base of the hill. He was turning around. I turned back to the fenced yards. I chose the chain link, figuring if it held a Doberman or Rottweiler at bay, by now the beast would be ripping at the fence in an effort to get at me. Now was the time I wished for a safety on my .38. It didn't even have a first click on it as a safety. If I had to use it as a club, the thing would probably discharge and give me away. Hastily, I ejected a cartridge and placed the hammer on the empty chamber.

I took a deep breath. "Okay, Tony. Go!" I yanked open the gate and raced across the yard, expecting an uproar. Uneventful seconds later, I vaulted the back fence and stumbled down the rocky slope and sprinted across the access road, hoping to lose myself among the homeless winos living under the Interstate.

I slowed to a walk, turned up my collar, and jammed my hands in the pockets of my jacket in an effort to blend into the clusters of aimlessly wandering winos and homeless men. Several accosted me, but I ignored them.

Four blocks ahead, the lights of the Green Light Parking Garage beckoned. Now that I had managed to shake his goons back at the cemetery, my next problem was how to reach Danny O'Banion without picking up a couple of rounds of slugs.

* * *

Austin is unique, a mélange of old and new. The older buildings, many constructed of the native white limestone, fill the city blocks on the periphery of the newer construction downtown. Alleyways, indigenous to the thirties and forties, crisscross the older city blocks, creating innumerable sleeping nooks for the homeless.

I shuffled into an alley, just across the street from the parking garage. I couldn't tell if any of Danny's buttonmen were watching or not, so I continued the role of a drunk and slumped into the darkness beside a dumpster, feigning sleep.

No one paid any attention.

Chapter Twenty-one

Long minutes passed as I sat in the darkness, peering at the garage from under my eyebrows, waiting for an opportunity, a suggestion as to how I could make it inside. Around two o'clock, a black limo pulled into the garage, but Danny's soldier refused to let the vehicle up the ramp. The driver jumped out and bellied up to the well-dressed goombah. I couldn't hear his words, but from his gesticulations, he was furious.

The soldier nodded, pulled out a cell phone and spoke into it. The gesture seemed to pacify the driver, who nodded to the vehicle.

A short time later, Danny, his collar unbuttoned and his red hair rumpled, appeared from an elevator, spoke briefly with the driver, who then returned to the limo and drove into the night. I waited until things had time to calm down before rising to my feet.

I stumbled across the street, my fingers wrapped about the Colt in my pocket. Staggering into the garage, I lumbered toward the goombah.

He shook his head when he spotted me. "Hey, lush. Beat it. You ain't sleeping it off in here."

He reached for my shoulder, but I spun his arm away and jammed the .38 under his chin. "Okay, buster. Not a word. Do what I say, and no one gets hurt." I nodded to the elevator. "Over there."

I had a sick feeling in the pit of my stomach. I couldn't back away now if I wanted.

Danny stared at me in surprise when I pushed his buttonman into the office ahead of me. Baby Huey jumped up from the couch and jammed his hand inside his coat.

I swung the Colt on him. "Hold it right there." From the corner of my eye, I glanced at Danny. "I don't want to hurt anyone, Danny. I just don't want them hurting me before I get a chance to talk. Understand?"

He hesitated, then gave a terse nod of his head.

Huey and the buttonman disappeared.

I studied Danny. The faint smile on his lips was overpowered by the icy glare in his eyes. Slowly, I laid the .38 on his desk and stepped back. "I meant it, Danny. I don't want to hurt anyone."

He glanced down at the Colt, then sat on the couch. He spoke, his tone crisp and business-like. "I can't let you leave here alive. You know that, don't you?"

"That what your bosses told you?" I crossed the room and stared out the window. The streets were empty, but that meant nothing. In the distance, an approaching storm sent flickers of light through the heavy clouds.

"Business is business, Tony. I told you not to stick your nose in something you didn't know anything about."

I turned back to him, chuckling.

He frowned. "Either you know something I don't, or you're a fool."

For some strange reason, I felt sorry for Danny. He had all the trappings of wealth, yet he was only a gopher, a well-paid one, but still only a gopher for his bosses. "I'm going to do you a favor, old friend."

He arched an eyebrow. "A favor? You're in not much of a position to be doing anyone a favor."

I sat on the corner of the desk and grinned at him. "I don't know how much your friends have invested in Chalk

Hills, but I can tell you this. Soon, by the end of July, they're going to lose every cent they have invested in the operation. And whatever the scandal will be, their names will be part of it."

Danny wore a good poker face, but still, I saw the involuntary twitch of an eyebrow indicating his surprise. I continued. "Now, you can waste me and keep me from proving Patterson was murdered. That won't stop whatever's going on out there."

He just stared at me with the eyes of a predator shark.

I continued. "William Cleyhorn, attorney for Chalk Hills Distillery, invested two hundred thousand on the gamble that the stock values would fall."

That got his attention. "Go on." He leaned forward.

"What do you know about calls and puts?"

"Calls and puts for what?"

"An investment strategy, Danny. Options. Risky, but if someone hits everything just right, they can make a king's fortune."

He looked at me in pained disbelief. "Is that all you got, stock market crap? Forget it."

"Forget eight million? Maybe even sixteen?"

Danny's eyes popped open.

I continued. "That's what Cleyhorn stands to gain if Chalk Hills' stock drops to twenty bucks a share. More if it drops lower. That's enough jack to make anyone take a chance."

"What are you talking about?" He shook his head, clearly puzzled.

"Look, Danny. There is an investment strategy available so that if you think a stock is going up, you can buy a *call contract* which gives you the right to purchase that stock at the strike price."

He stared at me blankly.

I started over, this time trying to keep it simple. "A contract gives you the right to buy or sell stock at a certain price. That price is the strike price. Follow me so far?"

He arched an eyebrow impatiently. "So what?"

"Okay. Now, if your strike price is fifty, and two months later, the share price is seventy, you can still purchase the stock for fifty. And you make twenty bucks a share. Understand?"

"Yeah. Go on." A faint frown knitted his eyebrows, but the first traces of understanding filled his eyes.

"A *put* is just the opposite. You purchase a contract which lets you sell stock at a given price—the strike price—regardless of the current value."

His frown deepened.

"Okay. Let me explain it this way. Cleyhorn bought the right to sell a hundred, maybe even two hundred thousand shares of Chalk Hills stock at a price of one hundred dollars a share. They're called July 100s, which means they mature at 11:59, Eastern Standard Time on Saturday following the third Friday of July. If, at that time, the shares are worth one hundred dollars each, he'll break even, but if the shares drop to twenty dollars a share, he'll sell at a hundred and make eighty bucks on each share." I paused. "Figure it out. Eighty times a hundred thousand. Eight mil. Twice that if he bought two hundred thousand."

Danny shook his head. "That doesn't make sense. From what you're saying, he's guessing that the distillery stock will fall."

I grinned. Little Danny O'Banion understood. "Exactly."

"But, why would he do that?"

I shrugged. "You tell me. Why would anyone invest two hundred thousand dollars on something like that? Two hundred thousand isn't the kind of money to gamble with. The only answer is that he knows something. And whatever that something is, it will cause Chalk Hills stock to drop clear down to the basement by the end of July."

He studied me several moments. "What does Cleyhorn have to do with Patterson?"

I chuckled wryly. "That I don't know. I stumbled across this stock market business when I was trying to find out who had reason to kill Patterson."

He puckered his lips thoughtfully. The chill faded from his tone. "You got proof of all this, Tony?"

I pulled out the fourteen pages I'd printed up. "Yeah. Here. Cleyhorn's financial records are in there." I handed them to Danny. I still had the disk. "I'm telling you, Danny, it's going to hit the fan. Sooner or later, your friends are going to take a soaking if they don't get out of Chalk Hills. Give this to them. Let them put their own investment counselors on it. Let them figure out why Cleyhorn spent two hundred thousand on a gamble that Chalk Hills would crash. If you don't, I'll guarantee you that they'll be coming after you first."

He studied me several seconds. "What's out there, Tony?"

I relaxed, slightly. The old conviviality was back in his voice. "Patterson was murdered. I know how the murder was done, and I think I know who did it. And I think I know why Patterson was blackmailing his killer. If I'm right, then there's another body at the distillery. And I think I know where it is."

Danny arched an eyebrow. "That's a lot of thinking."

"I know you figure Patterson got his money from drugs. But tell me this. How many dealers keep bank accounts in their own name? Huh? I'll tell you. Zilch. No, he got his money through blackmail. Take a look at those records. Every month for the last nine years, he made regular deposits above his paycheck. Prior to that, he didn't have a bank account. Like most of the laborers at Chalk Hills, he lived from paycheck to paycheck."

Danny arched an eyebrow. "A blackmailer with a bank account?"

"I thought about that, Danny. Now, Patterson was no rocket scientist, but he was certain his mark wouldn't stir up any trouble. So certain in fact, he had no fear of any incrimination from the bank account. Besides, the payoff deposits were in cash."

"So, who killed him?" Danny leaned forward.

I hesitated. "There's a chance I'm wrong about the killer,

but not about Cleyhorn. Like I said, have your bosses make him explain why he forked up two hundred thousand in a gamble that Chalk Hills stock would fall. This other, the Patterson business, give me some time. Everything I have is pure conjecture, but I believe it all points to the fact that Patterson witnessed a murder ten years ago. If I can get back to the distillery, I know where to find the body."

"What if there's no body?"

A cold chill swept over me. "I'm in big trouble."

Danny chewed on his bottom lip. "We're talking about my skin too, Tony. I'm not saying a word about this until you play out your hand. Let's see what you come up with." He paused. His eyes grew cold. "If you're right, I want to be the first to know. Understand?"

"Yeah, I understand."

"But, if you're not . . ."

Our eyes met, and his promise was explicit in his gaze. "I know."

"This is business. Nothing personal."

"I know."

With a grim shake of his head, he crossed the room and opened the door. "Huey will take you out there. He'll stop the others if they haven't got the word to lay off."

I reached for my Colt. "I might need this."

He arched an eyebrow.

With a chuckle, I shook my head. "Don't worry. It isn't for Huey. Probably wouldn't stop him anyway."

Danny chuckled. "Probably not."

Chapter Twenty-two

The storm approached the city. A few sprinkles of rain dotted the windshield of the Lexus as we wound out of downtown Austin. I had Huey pull into a twenty-four-hour convenience store where I purchased a couple of flashlights.

I paused at the telephone carrel beside the door and pulled Patterson's set of numbers from my pocket. I read through them, glanced at the keypad on the telephone, and jotted down the next set of numbers.

The drizzle grew heavier.

Back in the Lexus, Huey stared at me, puzzled. "What was the phone business?"

Taking a deep breath, I patted my shirt pocket. "I'm hoping this is where I find the final piece of the blackmail puzzle, Godz . . . I mean, Huey."

"I don't understand."

I nodded in the direction of the distillery. "You don't have to. Just drive." I hesitated. Maybe it wouldn't hurt to bounce my little theory off someone, even someone like Huey. I showed him the number: 2-91-147878969632. "You see this?"

He glanced at the numbers as he pulled onto the highway. "Yeah."

"Well, here's how it goes . . . I think. First, the two

indicates the rackhouse where they age whiskey. Ninety-one is the year the batch was put up for aging."

He laid a sausage-thick finger on the paper. "What's them other numbers?"

"A code."

"A code?" He frowned. "What kinda code?"

"Simple and smart, Huey. Simple and smart. Ls. The first four digits form an L on the keypad of any push button telephone. Starting with one, you have four, seven, then eight.

Then beginning at seven, the next L is seven, eight, nine, six. Then moving counter-clockwise to the next corner, the next four numbers make another L."

"That's the last of the numbers," he said, pointing to the 9632.

"Yeah. So, what's the next logical set of numbers?"

He frowned. "Huh?"

"Patterson was a puzzle freak. He played games with numbers, and that's what he did here." I showed him my notebook. "The next logical set of numbers is three, two, one, four. The next L on the keypad."

His eyes grew wide. "Yeah. I see what you're talking about. Hey, that's pretty slick."

I cautioned him. "If I'm right. And, if I am, we're looking for barrel number three thousand, two hundred and fourteen in the batch of whiskey barreled in 1991 and stored in Rackhouse Two."

He pursed his lips. "Why?"

I leaned back against the seat and stared out the window. "For the answer to this whole mess."

I crossed my fingers. If my hunch was wrong, I'd blown the whole caper. And Danny's bosses would see that I never had the chance to do it again.

The rain grew harder, and the windshield wipers thumped back and forth. Just ahead, lightning lanced at the ground.

* * *

Only a couple of security lamps lit the grounds of the otherwise dark distillery. I opened the glove compartment and reread the list of numbers, 2-91-147878969632. I stared at the four I had added, 3214. I shook my head at Patterson's ingenuity.

"Okay. Drive me to Rackhouse Two." I nodded to a distant building almost obliterated by the driving rain.

I glanced around, expecting lights to be flashing on as we drove up, but the distillery continued to slumber, except for a single lit window in the lab and the security light in front of the maintenance barn.

Through the window, I spotted the Massey Ferguson 230, and then I captured the tenuous thought that had been evading my grasp. I glanced at the ghostly bulk of the giant oak, and I knew exactly how the killer made his escape. And it wasn't hanging from a limb until the tandem disc passed.

Huey parked in front of the double doors and shut off the engine. I handed him a flashlight. "Get a tire tool and let's go."

He grunted.

I opened the door and made a dash for the rackhouse doors.

Moments later, he met me just inside the double doors, tire tool in hand. I shook the water off my head and shone the flashlight beam on the paper in my hand. "Like I said, here's the serial number we're looking for: 91-3214."

I headed for the first row of barrels, stacked in racks four high. Huey followed, surprisingly light on his feet considering his size. The flashlight beams slashed through the darkness like swords, settling on the white patch of paint on the first row of white oak barrels. "There. Ninety-four, six, five . . . must be a couple of rows over," I whispered. The next several rows were ninety-three, then ninety-two, and finally, fourteen rows over, ninety-one. My heart thudded in my chest when I focused the beam on ninety-one, one, zero, zero, zero.

The next row began at two thousand. "It's in the next

one over," I exclaimed. Sure enough, the first serial number was 91-3000.

I paused. What if I was wrong?

I shook my head. I wasn't wrong. It all fit together too neatly. With Huey on my heels, I hurried down the dark aisle of the cavernous rackhouse, the puny beam of the flashlight punching a tiny hole in the darkness ahead of us, illuminating the serial numbers. The rain drummed on the roof, ominous background music as we crept down the row.

Suddenly, I jerked to a halt. I centered the beam on the barrel in the third rack, almost head high. There it was, barrel 91-3214.

Huey whispered. "That it?"

I stared at the barrel, unable to believe I had actually found it; that there actually was a barrel with this number. I had to hand it to Patterson. He kept the barrel hidden for years by simply changing the year of production. I moved closer to study the serial number. If I was right, there might be some faint traces of black smudge against the white background.

To my disappointment, there was no indication of the year having been altered. But, it had to have been. I ran the beam of light along the barrel, noting the tight fit of the staves, the precision-like placement of the metal bands. I tried to imagine what was inside the barrel.

Outside, the lightning crashed.

I cleared my throat. "Yeah. I think this is it. Now, give me a hand. Let's turn the barrel until the bung is facing us."

Together, we managed to skid the barrel in the rack until the bung hole stared at us.

Overhead, the rain pelted the roof with a steady drumming.

Huey looked down at me. "Now what?"

I shook my head. I cocked my head back and stared up at the big man. "Now, we're going to find out if I'm a detective or a teacher with no future."

"Huh?"

"I'll explain later. There, the bung hole. Use the tire tool and knock out the plug."

He frowned, but Danny had him trained. Huey did exactly what I asked. With one sharp blow, he popped the plug loose.

Brown liquid spurted out on the dirt floor splattering mud on our trousers. Before I could say a word, a pale hand and thin wrist popped through the hole, abruptly halting the flow of whiskey."

"What the—!" Huey barked in surprise.

A crash of lightning reverberated throughout the rack-house.

I could only gape at the tiny, slightly wrinkled forearm protruding from the whiskey keg, its lightly colored flesh plugging the flow of whiskey.

I had found Katherine Voss.

I heart a faint pop, and Huey groaned and slumped to the ground. Behind me, whiskey spurted from another barrel through the hole punched in it by the slug.

I spun, but a beam of light blinded me. "Don't move an inch," said the voice, a familiar one.

Squinting into the light, I nodded slowly. "Forget about it. You don't stand a chance, Jackson. I know exactly what happened, and it's all on paper, even down to this barrel where you hid Katherine Voss ten years ago."

The light moved closer. "Shut up. Keep your light on the floor."

My beam shone on Huey, who lay motionless on the floor. Jackson nudged the prostrate man with the toe of his shoe. A stain of blood spread across Huey's chest. "This one won't bother anyone. Okay, now turn around."

I hesitated.

"Don't try it, Boudreaux. Don't try it. Now, turn around."

Reluctantly, I did as he ordered. He patted me down, finding the Colt in my coat pocket. "You won't need this," he said, dropping it into his own pocket. "Now, head for the door."

Outside, he pointed me toward the building that housed the Saladin Box. The rain fell steadily, soaking us. Raising his voice against the storm, he moved up close behind me. "Don't get brave. In this rain, nobody can hear a thing."

I kept waiting for lights to pop on around us, just enough distraction for me to try to get away, but as my luck would have it, Jackson was right. The windows remained dark. Either the storm was too noisy or everyone was sleeping.

One chance. When I stepped inside the unlit building, I would disappear into the darkness for an instant. That's when I had to make my play.

Jackson anticipated my move. Just as I reached the building, he jammed his automatic in my back. "Easy, now. Just take it nice and slow. I know what you're thinking. Believe me, you don't stand a chance."

The lights flashed on, illuminating the long, narrow building in a weak, yellow light. In the bay running the length of the building were the six huge corkscrews of the Saladin Box.

I needed time, time for something to happen. Just what, I had no idea. Jackson gave me the time.

"Well, Mr. Boudreaux. You've done that which I was never able to do."

I faced him. "Find the girl?"

"Yes, and now, thanks to your snooping, I'll be able to dispose of her, after which I will inform the police how you murdered your friend back there, and then fell in the Saladin Box when you were trying to kill me."

"Why the girl, Jackson? I know she came after the yeast, but why kill her over it?"

A trace of remorse edged his reply. "That was an accident. She stole the formula and tried to escape. She fell down the stairs outside my office and broke her neck."

"Why didn't you just tell the truth?"

"Why?" He laughed in disbelief. "You ask why? Chalk Hills, naturally. Stock prices had soared. We couldn't afford any scandal."

"You mean Morrison went along with you on the cov-erup?"

He shook his head. "No one knew. Except Patterson."

"You're a clever man, Jackson. Did you really plan your escape from the tractor, or did it just happen?"

His face was like granite, and his eyes were cold as death. "The world progresses, Mr. Boudreaux, because those of us who think can also plan, and make sure their plans succeed."

"Well, it was clever. But, I don't understand why you killed Patterson now, after so many years."

He gestured to the stairs leading to the walkway over the Saladin Box. "You're not as smart as you look. He was bleeding me dry. It wasn't so bad at first, but over the years, he wanted more and more. He didn't leave me any choice. So, I took a chance, and thanks to your snooping, I'll soon have my old life back."

I shook my head. "Don't count on it."

Jackson sneered. "Don't get your hopes up. No one is here. You can play for all the time you want, but to no avail. The old lady is in town, Tucker and Hawkins are on a binge, and nothing can wake Seldes or Runnels except four-thirty each morning."

I hesitated, but the nudge of his automatic sent me up the stairs. "I figured it all out, Jackson. Except one thing. The weapon. After you hit Patterson, you climbed up the tree and made your way back to the second floor window. A limb punched a hole in your cheek. That was the purpose of the Band Aid. My only question is what did you do with the club?"

His voice carried a lilt of amusement. "All of you walked right past it. In fact, some helpful soul even placed it back on the stack of logs."

I grimaced. I remembered that morning on the way to the distillery, I found a log of firewood on the ground and tossed it back on the stack. I was the helpful soul.

We reached the walkway at the top of the stairs. I hes-itated. He tilted the muzzle. "Over to the railing." At the same time, he flipped a switch, and with a deep humming groan, the eighty-foot corkscrews began turning, their six blades meshing. By the time the blades pushed a body eighty feet, nothing would be left but a bloody smear.

My brain raced. I glanced at the Saladin Box below. My only chance was to leap beyond the bay, almost twenty feet.

Suddenly, the door below slammed open. Huey staggered inside followed by a gust of rain.

Jackson shouted. "What the—"

Huey jerked his head up and in the same motion fired at Jackson, but the Master Distiller, Emeritus was a second faster. His slug spun Huey around, but that gave me the time I needed.

Lowering my head, I charged the taller man.

He spun back and fired just as I hit him. A powerful blow struck my side, throwing me off balance, but with one hand, I clung to Jackson, pulling him with me, at the same time scrabbling for his gun with the other. I grabbed his wrist and hung on like a turtle with his head cut off.

Grappling and biting, we rolled along the walkway. He tried to jam his knee in my groin, and I tried punching him in his temple. A numbness spread down my side into my leg.

"You cheap . . ." he muttered. "I'll . . ."

I butted him in the nose with my head and grabbed his wrist with both hands, at the same time, rolling him over and frantically slamming his hand against the iron walkway in a desperate effort to break his grip on the automatic.

In the next instant, he cursed, but the handgun clattered across the walkway and fell into the Saladin Box below. I was straddling his waist. Abruptly, I sat up and busted him between the eyes with my fist.

He caught me on the side of the head. Stars exploded, and my head slammed against the iron floor. I felt myself falling into a deep abyss.

I fought against the unconsciousness threatening me. If I passed out, I was dead. Groggily, I staggered to my feet, using the railing to steady my swaying body.

"You low-class hick," he growled, leaning forward at the waist, chest heaving, fists clenched. "I'm going to enjoy watching you die." He took a step toward me.

The wound in my side began burning, the pain radiating through my torso. I clutched the wound, hoping to ease the throbbing, but I kept my eyes on Jackson. He was desperate. He had nothing to lose. He had to kill me.

A cold determination settled over me. I was weak. I didn't know how long I could last, but whatever he got wasn't going to come easy. "Get on with it," I gasped.

With a maniacal gleam in his eyes, he lunged, and I swung a wicked uppercut, catching him flush on the chin and spinning him around. His veins must have been pumping nothing but adrenaline for Jackson bounced off the wall and leaped at me, fingers extended, all in one motion.

I screamed in pain as he drove them into my eyes. I grabbed him around the waist and slung him into the railing. Quickly, I backed away, blinking my eyes in a desperate effort to focus. My numbed leg threatened to fold on me.

Jackson snarled like an animal. He was a blur stalking toward me. With a shout, he leaped. "You're a dead man, Boudreaux!"

"Not yet." I leaned back against the wall for balance and kicked at him, catching him right in the groin.

He cried out in pain and doubled over, clutching his groin. He hit on the walkway and rolled back and forth violently in agony.

I blinked again, and when he came into focus, I shouted. "Jackson! Stop rolling! Don't . . ." I was too late. Alonzo Jackson, with a shriek of terror, rolled off the walkway into the Saladin Box.

Staggering to my feet, I stumbled the length of the walkway to the cutoff switch, falling half-a-dozen times before I reached it. The groaning corkscrews ground to a halt.

My legs gave way, and I sagged to the walkway.

I lost track of time. Somehow, I made it down the stairs to Huey, who was still alive, despite eating two slugs. I pulled his cell phone from his pocket and called Danny. I remember looking down at Huey when I clicked off the phone. He was grinning up at me.

The last thing that flickered through my mind was the field day Ben Howard and his cops were going to have with all this.

Chapter Twenty-three

I awoke in my own bed. I lay motionless, gazing at the ceiling and then around the bedroom, surprised to still be alive. I turned my head on the pillow and saw Oscar in the living room, still swimming in circles.

I tried to sit up, but the sharp pain in my side cautioned me otherwise. I moaned and lay back, closing my eyes.

"Well, Tony boy. You decided to come back to us, huh?"

I opened my eyes. Danny was looking down at me, a sandwich in one hand, a beer in the other, and a typical lopsided Danny O'Banion grin on his face.

"Hey." That was all I could say.

"Hey, yourself. How you feeling?" He took a bite of sandwich and washed it down with beer—Bud Lite, I noticed. I guess he didn't like my Old Milwaukee.

"How . . . how'd I end up back here? What about—"

He held up the sandwich, silencing me. "Everything's taken care of. Nothing for you to do or worry about."

I tried to focus my thoughts. He laughed at the contortions on my face, and sat on the edge of the bed.

"Just relax. I'll bring you up to date. First, you've made yourself a number of very influential friends, who, naturally, do not wish their names to be spread around." He paused while he took a huge bite from one corner of the sandwich, chewed it up, gulped it down, and chugged a

197

couple of swallows of beer. "But, you saved them money and notoriety. The first they want, the second, they don't. They won't forget you, Tony."

I managed to prop myself up on one elbow. Wincing, I asked, "But, what about Huey, and Jackson?"

Danny took another bite of sandwich. "Huey's fine. He's a rock. He told us what took place. We cleaned everything up. Jackson, unfortunate accident. He stumbled and fell. It'll have a couple of paragraphs on the back pages. We've seen to that. The Voss girl? We sent her back to her father."

He saw the question on my face, so he quickly explained. "We told him she had been in the morgue here, unidentified."

"For all those years?"

He gave me a look of innocence. "Go down and look at the records. They're there for everyone and anyone to see."

I stared in disbelief at my old high school chum. I shook my head, leaned back, and chuckled. "Jeez, Danny. Isn't there anything you can't take care of?"

He polished off the sandwich and the rest of the beer. "Not a thing." Then he belched. "By the way. Your boss, Marty . . . whatever his last name is, well, Marty said for you to take a couple of days to heal the cuts you got when the horse you were riding threw you into a barbed-wire fence."

I shook my head in disbelief. They'd even changed the way I got hurt. What next? "Oh, he did, did he?"

Danny laid his hand on my shoulder.

"He's not a bad guy, Danny. For a jerk."

We both laughed. Or, rather, he did. I grimaced at the tenderness in my side. The wound from the barbed wire sure hurt.

A frown wrinkled Danny's forehead. "I got a question, Tony. How did you figure all that out? About Jackson and the girl, I mean. That was some slick detective work."

I gave him a silly grin. It felt good having someone brag on you, but the truth was, it was nothing but dogged perseverance. I shrugged. "Little things that didn't quite fit. A

Band Aid on a simple razor cut for a week? More like a limb punched a hole in his cheek. Then he claimed he couldn't fire Patterson, yet Morrison herself told me she never interfered. One of the two lied. No reason for her, so it had to be him. That meant there had to be another reason he didn't get rid of the guy. And then he said Patterson was drunk that Sunday. There was no way he could have known that."

"Somebody could have told him."

"Could have, but no one did. I asked. But what really tripped me to the fact Jackson was lying was when he said Voss was wearing a white blouse. That, and a bank account that didn't match his income."

Danny's frown deepened. "But the girl was wearing a white shirt when we took her out of the barrel."

"Yes, but not the first time. You see, when Jackson first saw her, she had on a red blouse. He sent her to Seldes, and that's when Seldes found her and Patterson going at it like two rabbits. When Seldes refused her a job, she went back to Jackson, but first she changed her shirt right in front of poor old Tom Seldes."

I hesitated, thinking how simple it was now that I knew all the details. "Jackson swore she never came back, but he stated she wore a white shirt."

"I see." Danny's face lit up. "If she hadn't gone back to him, there was no way he could have known she was wearing a white shirt."

I pointed my finger at him and winked. "Pow. You got it. The other stuff . . . well, the truth is, it came to light because everything else was eliminated. But, I was sidetracked by the blow to the back of Patterson's head."

Danny frowned.

"The Medical Examiner's office said the blow appeared to be delivered by a woman. That threw me until I realized how difficult it would be to balance on a moving tractor and swing a club at the same time. No way a man could put his whole weight into the swing."

He shook his head and lit a cigarette. "Well, you done good, chum. You done good."

"What about Cleyhorn?"

"You were right. He was going to skip the country. He knew about the blackmail because Alonzo Jackson had borrowed from Cleyhorn to keep Patterson quiet. That gave the shyster the idea about breaking the company's back and making a fortune. Can you imagine the scandal? Body discovered in whiskey vat after ten years. Who wants to drink Chalk Hills Bourbon after a body has been found pickled in one of its casks?"

"The stock would have dropped to zero." I paused, uncertain if I should ask the next question. What the heck, I told myself. They won't waste someone who saved them millions. "Where is lawyer Cleyhorn now?"

The smile faded from his face. "Don't ask." He glanced at Oscar. A wry grin twisted across his face. "Hey, why not? You Catholic?"

"Yeah. Well, sort of. Why?"

"Nothing. I was just going to suggest if you were Catholic, you might make the sign of the cross whenever you take the new exit ramp off three-sixty to Bee Tree Road."

All I could do was stare.

Danny winked. "How about a beer?"

My mouth was dry, but I had no desire for a beer. I don't know if it was because of old Gus down at the Riverside Club, or the stress of my healing. "No, thanks. A glass of water'll do."

He nodded. "I'll get you one, then you get some sleep. That's the best thing for you."

I leaned back, wondering what my old man would have to say about the job I had done. Probably find something to sneer at. I shook my head. Who cared?

I closed my eyes. As I drifted off, I made a mental note to send the snapshots back to Tom Seldes. Next, I'd call Janice and promise her some blackened redfish and an exciting evening if she'd forgive me.

Then, like Danny had said a couple of days earlier, all would be right with the world.